# Anonymous
# Nude Photos

Lauren Jane K.

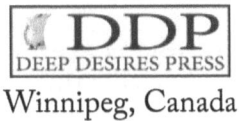

DDP
DEEP DESIRES PRESS

Winnipeg, Canada

Developmental editor: Margaret Larson
Proofreader: Francisco Feliciano

Published April 2023 by Deep Desires Press, an imprint of Story Perfect Inc.

Deep Desires Press
PO Box 51053 Tyndall Park
Winnipeg, Manitoba R2X 3B0
Canada

Visit http://www.deepdesirespress.com for more scorching hot erotica and erotic romance.

Subscribe to our email newsletter to get notified of all our hot new releases, sales, and giveaways! Visit deepdesirespress.com/newsletter to sign up today!

# Anonymous
# Nude Photos

# 1.

If I am honest, I don't remember the first time I saw him because this is not a fairy tale. At first, he was only a detail suppressed into the background. I photographed his work for agents, auction houses, websites. We moved in connected circles: artist and documenter. The truth of him was hidden among the tangle of his installations, the busy days of shooting several pieces. I saw him only through a professional distance. I would look over his sculptures the same way I looked over all the art I photographed, noting only the play of light over shape and form, composition, space and blocking. At first, he was hardly more than a figure that cast a shadow. He deflected light traced over tattooed skin when he rolled up his sleeves, he moved silently in the background while agents hovered around the lens, tossing light around.

We barely spoke, mostly words relating to position in space. Left. Right. Forward. Thirty degrees, forty-five. Brighter. Darker. Over. Under. Entire conversations in single words. Cryptic to anyone listening: the account managers and agents, maybe even some of the interns. We didn't speak at all. Perhaps I should have noticed our easy understanding. It's so rare to not need to say very much to be understood. But I didn't. I liked his art more than most though. Quality or personal subjective opinion was always beside the point of my presence, but sometimes a piece would stand out. Shine. And his would glimmer.

Once I shot a headshot of him for an auction brochure featuring contemporary works. Innocent of the future's intentions, I watched him through the jaw snap of my shutter, arms crossed or tattooed hands in motion, the twist of rope and shadow as he strung up his sculpture, a flock of cow skeletons, blown apart in exploded isometric diagram. Suspended. He was beautiful, he moved well. But I saw him, at the time, much the same way I saw one of his pieces. I watched the space he took up. I didn't know the hands I watched would one day tie me to the sky, put me on my knees, force me there, that I would kiss his palms, warm from slapping my face.

How could anyone know something like that was waiting for them...


Every now and then you go somewhere, or you do something, and you don't know you are beginning a series of events that will change your life, change everything about you. It was an Artist's opening in the Brickworks' dilapidated back rooms, hidden in a hollow valley of Toronto. Large, vivid canvases on thin stands screaming out in splashes of neon paint, photos lashed to wood with heavy strokes of varnish. The naked brick walls were warm and red, the open space filled with voices in a low simmer of sound. I wandered around with my camera.

Along the factory's northern wall crumbling old brick ovens, long narrow spaces separated by thick walls, the arching ceilings and chimneys long vanished or crumbling. At the end of each tunnel, films were shining from projectors. I chose one that looked not too crowded and wandered in, leaning against the wall near the back, as far away from the rows of chairs as possible.

Except in this one, there wasn't a film. There was him.

Dressed in a black collared shirt with the sleeves rolled up, moving around with coils of rope, ignoring the audience who were sitting around on a tufted leather sofa and thick fur rugs. At first, I took out my camera and simply held it on the two bodies he was tying. He moved in and out of frame on the end of the rope tether, winding it around the bodies of two people dressed in spools of silk. I wondered if he tied them into the dresses as well. I held the tied bodies in the center of my frame.

As the tie went on, I focused less on the finished product of the bind, on the women now embracing, and more on him. As the rope moved through escalating complexity I focused more on the motion of the material, the bend and fly of the rope, the process of movement and touch. After a while, though, I put down the camera and simply watched. I hardly saw him before. But I liked what he did, the things he made and this, taut lines around flesh.

I lifted the camera again and watched him more carefully through the snap of the shutter of the lens. The twist of rope, the fall of light and shadow as he strung one of the models up in the air, made her a decorative object, held aloft by rope like a floating isometric diagram, skin and jute origami. Hindsight calling in her siren voice, a trick of memory and time.

When I developed the photos, they were striking, busy and angular. Dark. They were some of my best photos in a long time. No matter what their sensuality suggested, I didn't know the hands I watched would one day so soon touch me, tie me, make me cry. As I took the photos, it didn't even occur to me to wonder.

Eventually, though, I'd find out we'd been circling each other around the city for years. We went to the same tattoo parlor, visited the same cafe when we wanted to be alone, we once shared an unknowing dinner in a late-night neon diner in Toronto after a concert we both attended. The coincidences spilled over into other cities. We both made sure to visit MarieBelle's chocolate shop every time we were in Manhattan, went to the same English bookstore in Berlin. Coincidences scattered around us. There are more, I'm sure. Ones we don't know and will never discover. I should have known, watching him tie bodies into space.

I should have known.

He found me after the performance was over. I'd moved back toward the wetland trails behind the brick ovens, wandering on the boardwalk, he appeared behind me just when I thought myself alone, his voice low in the din.

"I know you…"

I turned, heart pounding, trying not to seem startled.

"I saw you while I was…" he gestured over his shoulder. "Well. I liked working with you. You photographed *7744*, remember?"

I nodded as though only just remembering, but I could never forget *7744*, a powerful sculpture. A piano in 7744 pieces hanging in a tense mid-explosion. It took sixteen hours to assemble.

"You shot everything dead straight. You hardly moved. I remember one of the agents saying it was as if you were only interested in the perspective of the most unimaginative person of the room."

I laughed; I hadn't been expecting to and almost tripped over the sound, trying to hide it behind a nod.

"He wasn't wrong," I said, and he laughed then as well and nodded.

"It was a pleasant change. Most of the photographers I see for these types of things want the photo to represent the feeling of the work. Making art from art."

I shook my head.

"I'm just there to operate a machine; the work needs to be itself, not what I think it is. The photos are disingenuous otherwise. Dishonest. Your piano wasn't going to work, anyway. No matter how creative I was, I wasn't going to be able to get the piece in a photo."

"How so?"

Sometimes, you get lucky and hit on some hidden secret combinations of words that make someone open up. Nothing about him changed, but he was paying more attention; I could feel it like a shift of the current in the air.

"The piece was about perspective," I said carefully. "The thing isn't a piano from any perspective. You have to walk through it to see it, to understand it. Motion is implied."

I took a sip of water, unable to think of anything else to say, but this seemed to be enough. He looked over the crowd behind us, but everything about his gaze was internal.

We were silent for a long time. I thought of something to say.

"Pianos have over 12,000 individual pieces."

"Pardon?" He looked at me, and his gaze made me feel uneasy, too aware of myself somehow.

"I looked it up after. 12,000 pieces."

"I know. It's just…that's interesting. That you looked it up" He smiled. "When did you know you wanted to photograph art. It must be a constricting field."

"I didn't decide. It was something I started doing to be close to the community without actually being in it. It just became this whole thing." I waved my hand dismissively. "An accidental career."

"How do you mean?"

"There is a period of accommodation, you know, after university but before you are formally and officially *the thing you do*. A real job, a real place to live, instead of doing what you really want to do."

I raked my hand through my hair, phishing it off my face and then used both hands to hold my glass.

"And what did you really want to do?"

"What I really wanted to be was an artist." I waved my hand dismissively again, closed it in a fist when I realized I'd just done that, tried to close the conversation by lowering my voice. I hated this admission, and I worried his first impulse would be patronizing. It was a difficult and complex thing to admit to this man, to an artist, that I wasn't an artist, that I wanted to be one.

"Art is a verb. It is something you do."

The expression on his face was serious. I wondered at

the life that brought this man into existence, what tangle of events and timelines could have created him, brought him here, wandering in a manicured swamp, on the edge of a party he seemed to have forgotten.

"You must tell me about your work."

"No." I smiled softly, carefully. "I want to hear about yours. We can talk about me another time," I said, feeling bold enough to presume there might be another time. And I realized, in saying it, I wanted very much to see him again.

"I am thinning of starting something new. But my next project it needs to be something." He hesitated, looked me overcarefully and then out over the dark wetlands. He sighed. "Something really beautiful. And well, it's on a different scale."

"Scale?"

"More personal, maybe." He looked at me for a long time again. "I'm looking for space, and I'll need new tools." His copper eyes sparkled in the dark as he smiled, focus still intent. He produced his phone from his breast pocket with a simple gesture; a fold of his wrist, the kind of motion that suggested a weapon.

"I'm sending my contact info to the number I had for you from the agency. I want you to call that number in three days. At five." His voice dropped an octave, took on the sound of sandpaper, thorns. My phone buzzed in my pocket, the incoming contact waiting for my approval to nestle itself in my phone, find its place in the rank and file of the alphabet.

"Do you understand?"

I nodded, my throat so dry I doubted I would be able to speak. I had no idea what just happened to me.

Three days. And how to fill them. Summer was slow at work. The people who liked art auctions also enjoyed horse racing and garden parties, social functions under tents with summer wines and sailboats. I travelled less and found the sudden attention on three days, open and empty before me, glaring. In the ease of our conversation, I'd forgotten while we talked what drew us together, and remembering made my body come alive. My hands tingled with a kind of shock, like someone whispering you're name when you think you are alone.

I tried to be logical about it, to break up seventy-two hours into smaller and smaller pieces. Reducing it to measurable fragments of time. And even in doing so, knocking off hours for sleep and dinner, extended visits with friends, a few hours with my camera. I knew I would sleep poorly, that I would be distracted over cups of coffee, distant, quiet, that I would sit at my computer editing my photos but unable to focus on the work.

I hated the phone and longed to send a text instead. Neatly stacked pixels doing what my voice could not. But he said call, and I waited for five to appear on my clock. I thought of the rope, the stark nakedness of its lines, the sound of his voice just behind me, dark, moving like a stingray.

—*I know you…*

# 2.

He walked into the dark cafe as hot chocolate slid off my spoon into my mouth. He smiled, and I wondered later if it was because I did. He was beautiful, he moved like a cat through the dark cafe. It was the strangest feeling, relief and alarm at once. An unmistakable but mysterious moment of recognition. What went through my mind, as clearly as if I said it aloud, was:

*Of course. I should have known.*

At first, I could hardly speak. He talked about his work, his last project, a lush garden, a jungle made out of glittering shards of mirrors: elaborately carved birds with bodies made of dripping labia and splayed lilies and tulips, trees and mirrored flowers fashioned out of scrap metal, silvery vines of varnished clothesline and handwoven silver chains, everything precisely and impeccably made. A vision of hell and paradise, the otherworldly, the beautiful.

I could tell he was confident, passionate about the idea. But he was also wary, observing me carefully. His hands were scarred, curled around a mug of hot chocolate, the lick of a tattoo crossing up over his thumb.

"Can I see what you're working on?"

He shook his head. "My next project isn't really started yet. It's only and ideas. Things I'm imagining." He smiled at me, and it made my heart race a little faster. "Keeping me sane."

I thought about the slanted plane of darkness where I

developed film, the shape of my body in the photos I make, my body and the image folded carefully into existence. Secrets. I nodded.

*I'm the same.* I wanted to say, but I didn't. I didn't have the courage to compare myself to him. Instead, I asked, "What other things keep you sane?"

"I do what you saw before. I tie. I make people feel things."

With a perfection motion he grabbed my wrist, and I was caught in his fist. He squeezed, not hard but firm so I could feel the edges of my bones against his grip. He smiled a wicked wolf's grin. That smile. Brutal and terrifying and beautiful all at once. As if he actually wanted to hear me whimper, hurt me. And then it was gone, a flash of something glimpsed in dark water and let me go, rested his hand on my wrist gently for a moment.

"Tell me about you. About your art. That's twice now you deflected my question."

I flexed my hand on the table. I practiced my answer to this question, but now had no idea what I wanted to say.

"I used to paint massive canvases. But they got smaller and smaller. Eventually I stopped painting when I started working with a camera. Now I take self-portraits, stark, minimalist. Mostly black and white." I wanted to say so much more, about using the photos to find the limits and boundaries of myself, trying to see myself from everywhere at once. But I worried it would make no sense. So, I said nothing.

Instead, I talked a little about my photos of buildings, the minimal abstract landscapes. Origami photos of light, large scale printed photographs of architecture I took when I travelled for work and edited into complex patterns of symmetry that sometimes looked like spaceships. I showed him some of the finished photos on my phone.

"They are huge, though," I said. "And I make the composites by hand, paste up like old newspapers. No computers at all."

"I can see it, the scale. The way you describe them. You will have to show me some of the finished pieces. Where are you showing them?"

I blushed, looked away. "I don't." I said, my voice closed like a fist, and he nodded. We sat in the cafe, drinking hot chocolate, stumbling over unexpected common ground. Soon, I was so lost in conversation I felt as though I could crawl across the table and lick words off his lips as he said them. His voice was cut clean, as though slashed into space with a knife. It was night by then, deep into it, and I was not spared from night's hallucinations.

Lust.

Blood lust.

Excusing myself for a moment I slid out of the pew and left the table, made my way down the restaurant's too narrow stairs to the basement bathroom. Pressing my hands against the cool tile wall in the little bathroom I felt it warm under my flushed palms. I wanted to come right there, slide my hands down…

I wondered how only a voice could make me so wet, flush with want. Ready, even then, for a man who was basically a stranger. If he walked into that tiny bathroom, I would not fight him. I would not stop him. I would let hm take me and come in that hard profound way you can when you get exactly what you need. My mouth tasted like chocolate.

"I am thinking of renting a space." He said when I got back to the table. "But the one I like is too big, too much space for one person. It's better to share, perhaps?"

"Yes, perhaps." I said it before I understood what he was saying. Offering. Was he offering? I realized as soon as I spoke, I didn't really know. He only smiled. Suddenly the entire evening was worth it, the sign of empty cups and drawn-out silence meant something, and we could get up and leave our little table, separate into the wet, dark night.

Outside on the sidewalk, he put his hand on my shoulder.

"Come with me to see the studio. Monday afternoon? I will message you."

"Yes," I said again.

Quickly.

Again.

The studio he'd found was deep on a mostly abandoned strip of waterfront. We walked together from the subway during a cold spring rain, so close our arms almost touched. For a time, we moved in silence, listening to the white noise of the city, traffic, the constant sigh of sewer grates. The sound of rain was all around us for miles and miles in the empty industrial park. The afternoon storm was diluted by sunlight pressing against the clouds, a strange yellowish-green glowing off the pavement. The grit and the dust that drifted through the city glimmered in the rain.

A long chain-link fence stretched out beside us as we followed the slow curve of train tracks, bright with a steel shine, a radiating note of greenish black. The path was lined with small bones, curved ribs of small animals, dishwashing cotton, knitting wool, tape and ribbon, shreds of tin cans, bright foil and newspaper all wound up together and strung along by the wind like giant owl pellets or abstract sculptures.

We passed smokestacks blackened halfway down their towering stalks, silent now, burned-out lots made me think of cremation grounds. The smell of the death of industry was here, Ash and concrete dust, the hulking dry fragrance of rubble.

"These places were abandoned by industry over the past twenty or thirty years, as the heart of the city moved north to the suburbs. They made so many odd things, glove and button factories, pool tables." I said softly.

"It seems right then, doesn't it, that we make art out here. That things still get made here," I said. His smile made me flush with warmth, and I looked away.

A short time later, we came across the warehouse. The building loomed, blotting out the strange light. Crumbling brick and lines of square windows, opaque with grime. Once, this place produced billions of tiny buttons, beads, glass pendants and dolls eyes, so the litter in the lot was dusted with confetti of bright shards and scraps of glass orbs. The air still harbored a lingering sour smell of melted glass.

Even by day, the building looked abandoned, the windows dark, the grounds around it littered with glittering city dust. He took my hand, his grip firm as he led me toward a dented metal barn door on rusted rails. I felt no misgivings even though a small voice whispered: *You should be afraid....*

The thought tasted like knowledge. I had reason enough to suspect him. One moment he wasn't there, and the next, he was. A compelling presence, shining a dark light. A man I knew but didn't really know, who had taken me to an empty warehouse. All reasons to be on guard. But I couldn't summon a sense that his grip on my wrist was wrong or misplaced. I let him lead me inside even as I felt the violence in the strength of his hands. We stepped into the dim of a tall space filled with the crisscross of light and metal of a staircase and all I wanted was to close my eyes and feel more of his touch.

The building was a sprawling warren of space I could only glimpse through the industrial lattice of the stairwell. At the landing of each floor hung massive doors rollers. I followed him up the stairs. orange bulbs shed dusty light on our shoulders, sparkled with rain. It was cool, and the spatter and rattle of rain on the windows in their old metal frames made everything feel brittle. We arrived at the fifth floor, making our way down a long hallway, another barn door at the end of it, this one made out of sheets of green metal with wide fists of rivets.

"I hope you like it." He said it like a confession, hand

lightly on my wrist again, and I was afraid he would feel the thrum of excitement through my skin. He paused and spun the padlock on the door and slid it open with a hollow metal clang.

"It is perfect, I think. Enough space, more than enough, for two. And the light…"

I could see right away he was right. It was perfect. A long narrow space with impossibly high ceilings. Cool and empty. Wet windows ran along every wall, glass in a black iron grid, the space was filled with a pale white light. The rattling of the glass was alive, the building was breathing. At the end of the room was a door, the unmistakable red bulb of a dark room over a blacked-out window on a dark doorway.

"The darkroom is about 250 square feet."

"How is there a darkroom here?"

He shrugged. "Apparently a sales department, they did paste up on catalogues in here. You'll need to source an enlarger from somewhere, but there is plumbing, power, running water."

"It's perfect," was all I could say.

He smiled and I stopped questioning why he wanted me, a non-artist he just met, whose work he hadn't really seen. If I thought about it, it didn't make any sense. Why would he want me there at all? I knew it was quite possibly a mercenary invitation and he was looking to cut the rent, or maybe it was a matter of happenstance, convenience, perhaps he was hoping our paths would not cross much at all. It didn't matter. It was perfect.

We signed the lease on the paint-splattered metal ledge

built into the long wall under the windows, emailing our signatures to the listing agent. It was almost dark when we left, drizzling still, but we stood on the pavement for a while, looking up at the building. He reached out again, held my wrist. Hard. Pulled me to him in a hug, pressing me against the span of his chest. The crush of his arms enclosed me in the darkness of another person, almost a stranger, but still familiar.

He turned his face into my hair, felt him take a deep calm breath, as though breathing me in. I felt these things, my mind frozen, but my body answered with a tremble of its own, my hands, fingers curled, resting lightly on his shoulders. I wanted to look up at him, but I didn't. I couldn't move.

When he pulled away, it was sudden. His expression unreadable, as he looked at me, brow knit, and I felt as though he was studying me for something. Looking for something or watching for something. I looked down at my small black shoes, brushed my hair from my face and I could feel strands uncoil from my damp cheeks.

"Before I knew we would come here, I was planning it for months, renting this space for myself. But I felt...not ready somehow? It wasn't until I told you about it that it felt like the time to begin."

"I know," I said this, bravely, smiling, because what I meant was: *I felt it when I saw you. I thought, now. Now I am ready.*

But I didn't actually know if I was, or what I ready for. Still, I said it. *I know.*

I never wanted to show my art to anyone. I hesitated

even to call it art to myself. To think of my photos as art, my art. Showing art, sharing it, using it to tell a story, had always been, when I thought of other people's work, a significant part of the context for art. Art was made to be experienced, but revealing what I created was just not in the terms I established for myself. The drive to fold light into new shapes and configurations was really the drive to create, complete, to make something. Anything. Anything at all…

What I made was less important than the fact I made it. My self-portraits were a desire to create collapsed into a flattened state, creation with only my camera and myself, paper and a knife, and in the end was work I hardly saw as the sum of its parts.

More than showing my work, I wanted to have someone get it. And, I thought, watching him search me in the storm light in the dim of the warehouse, wondered if he would, if he could watch the scoring and folding, the careful razor-sharp carving away and rebuilding of shapes and think they were beautiful.


Walking back from the subway to my apartment, the padlock combination tucked away in my phone, I decided I'd set myself up to be got, or not, regardless. He would see the work. He would see everything: the stacks of photographs, the little cup of razor blades and paring knives and awls, my chocolate brown glass pots of glue and little rubber brushes always a little sticky. He would be able to look at, to touch, my film, the photo paper, my camera. It struck me as intimate.

That night in bed I thought of leaving myself naked and open on the paint-splattered table for him to look over with mild curiosity, as though my body were a brush or blade, a useful but common object. I let my hands slide over my breasts and belly. With a neatness of touch and an expert subtlety I mastered over years of lustful isolation, I sucked at my fingers slowly. Saliva ran into my mouth as I closed my eyes and imagined wetness growing between my legs, willed it there through synchronous pulses of tongue and cunt, two sets of suckling lips.

Carefully, wet fingers moved across my breasts, down my stomach, slipping between the lips of my cunt, my other hand moving to my mouth, my hand as active as my tongue, my thighs soon as wet. Pleasure curled, its edges folding in lacy wisps, it danced in a variety of the rhythms I tried; the easy slide, the lightest touch, my fingers sliding toward the calling darkness inside me. My body flexed and kneaded, all of me open to the lightest teasing of air, my body singing in the half-dark. As I came, I felt all the heat of his voice and as I sighed out my orgasm, I could smell the damp of spring rain in the warehouse district.

"You seem happy." Ruby poured frothing coffee from a percolator on her stove into wide mugs and added steaming sweetened oat milk, beaming as she handed me the huge blue cup. Sitting down across from me, she swung her legs up under her on the kitchen chair and pushed her fire engine red hair out of her face, sweeping it up in a knot with an easy twist of her wrist. A motion I never failed to find attractive and seductively feminine.

"I am." I smiled, an easy expression this morning. "I rented a studio."

Putting down her cup, she sat back in her chair. A look of mock amusement on her face was broken by a laugh.

"What? finally. That's excellent news. I'm so pleased for you." She smiled and kissed my forehead. "Have a cookie."

Lifting a cookie off the plate at the center of the table, she nudged the plate across the table at me.

"It seems so sudden. You hadn't even mentioned you were thinking about it."

"I wasn't. It just sort of happened."

"How did it just sort of happen?" A brow arch and I smiled. she was right, it was out of character. So, I told her about the art show, recognizing him from his work. I told her about the offer over coffee, the walk in the rain. I didn't say anything about how he made me feel, how our meetings seemed full of fate and secrets. Charged. How the last few nights I made myself come thinking about him tying me down in an empty warehouse, violence and moonlight in his voice.

But I told her how exhilarating the space was, the perfect light and echoing lofty ceilings. The small dark room with its shallow sinks. I didn't say anything about the hard clench of want I felt around him, like a magnetic pull. Something cellular, a trick of the blood. But in telling her the story, I could hear it in my voice. Untempered. Unmeasured. Unleashed. When I was done, she was still for a moment, then she stood and summoned me out onto her balcony.

Standing outside in the shade of the balcony above her she lit a joint and blew the smoke over the city. Rain threatened to begin again, and I smiled while Ruby frowned. The downspouts off the balcony above her still dripping. The trees below were glistening and dark.

"Tell me. What is this actually about?"

She crossed her arms and shook her head, so the strands of hair that escaped her bun were kicked back in the wind. She held the smoke in her lungs for a moment and let it out with a sigh; the wind ripped it away in long tatters. She passed it to me, but I shook my head.

"What do you mean?"

"This whole thing, it's not really about the studio. Or only about the studio. I mean, it's fabulous. It's amazing you have finally done it. It's the best decision you've made for yourself in a long time. Since you took this job. But you'd made up your mind before you went there, hadn't you?"

I thought for a moment, accepted the joint the second time she offered it and took a long, careful draw, tasting its sweetness. I crossed my arms, still holding the joint and looked out over the city.

"Yes." I realized, smiled, handed the joint back, shaking my head. "I suppose I had."

"So, if it's not about the actual studio, then what is it about?" She raised her finely drawn eyebrows and smiled, sly, like a fox.

I shrugged and laughed, breathing out smoke. "I couldn't say. There are no words to describe it."

And anyway, even if there had there been words, I wouldn't have said them. Even if there was a way of not revealing too much, even with Ruby, I didn't want to reveal anything. I wanted this to be mine alone, a secret.

"I'm excited by the idea. That's all."

"Of him, or the place?"

"Does it matter? Is it not enough just to be happy?"

She took the joint when I offered it and narrowed her eyes at me, a smile still playing over her lips now.

"Enough." She smiled, bumped her shoulder into mine softly. "What is enough?"

"We'll have to wait and see, I guess."

# 3.

Down a glittering street, slick with rain and haze, I walked beside him to the studio, our pace matched, hands in our pockets. When he hugged me hello at the subway station I pulled away, unsure. My body humming so hard I was afraid he would feel the beat of my heart, like a bird trapped in my chest, fluttering against my bones. He was so unknowing of the self that lurked inside, snapping heart in darkness.

Hunger.

Lust.

During my first few days in the darkroom, I had to actively renounce him from my thoughts. It was useless. I thought of him constantly. Despite myself, I would follow wild roads through my imagination, around the edge of the unknown, and find myself thinking about him as I worked in the darkroom and as I made the photos. I thought of him tying me to the rafters as I hung dripping film on the line like wet black ropes.

To keep from seeming as focused on him as I was, I spent most of my time ignoring him even as I was alive with happiness to be so near him. Throughout the last cool drift of spring, I found each day more perfectly illuminated than the last.

Those days I often bought myself flowers and worked mostly from bed, photographing myself with sleep lines still on my skin, the imprint of my bedsheets. I would shoot all morning, unwinding in front of a pool light, flowers pulled open. In the afternoons, I went to the little cafes with the round copper top tables. I drank tea and sparkling water. When we were apart, if I was away shooting something or if he was out at a show, I would miss our hours of quiet working. I doubted if anyone could look at the collection of my days and know the scope of my happiness, know how ornate and complete my happiness was in those simple hours.

I made so many photos. Every day I worked on photography making myself more real in increments of stolen time. When I photograph myself, it is essential somehow to the process to involve a physical element, a metaphor beyond my nudity or almost nudity. My body, my nudity had the impact of adding a seemingly endless awareness of sex. But in photography is never just about sex, nothing I photographed was just about sex either, even if it was a photo of my body spread open, held open by many hands. I would use black ink or ribbon, knives, long lengths of chain or wire. The objects added tension, a non-sexual element suddenly charged. These things became about power, expectation, pain, comfort or discomfort.

All photographs are memories, even if they aren't candid. To make a photograph is to participate in your or another person's or object's mortality, vulnerability, mutability. To make a photograph is to participate in reality, to be a member of the world, to create part of it. Even if you never show it to anyone. When I see my scars and tattoos in a photo, I remember a former or current self, proof I have been someone all this time. I lived in a near-constant state of creative arousal, and craving the company of my work, went to the studio almost every afternoon to develop my film from the morning.

He spent entire days at the studio, while I trailed in near late afternoon, after visiting a gallery or studio for work. I liked to arrive before the blue light of evening, when the shadows were long and tinged with darkness, that soft but glorious summer light. One day I arrived, and he'd laid down a rug made of tightly knotted black rope and moved in two overstuffed armchairs and a low metal coffee table. After a few weeks we had collected an array of chipped mismatched teacups, jadeite coffee mugs. My side was empty but for a massive drafting table, a narrow stool, a banker's lamp. No decoration but the fall of light from my banker's lamp, the strips coiled of paper falling around the table legs, ribbons of uncurling film drying.

"Spartan." He called it with a smile I could not name or place.

I loved its emptiness, its light, I even loved his cups scattered about, ringed with coffee grounds or turpentine. I would smile at a sweater forgotten on a chair, black and shapeless, not knowing if it was his or mine.

One evening I brought pastry, two cinnamon rolls and little loaf of fresh bread, some cheese, two pears. He smiled that same smile, already starting the water to boil as I slid the door open on its hard steel wheels. Steam rose between us as he poured water over coffee grounds. The coffee steeped, and I watched him lick cinnamon off his fingers.

"Why self-portraits?" He asked.

The coffee was strong. He often made it almost too strong to drink but it was good with the sweetness of the cinnamon. I didn't answer for a long time, but he didn't say anything else, seemingly happy to wait. We looked out a large grid of windows, sky carved up into neat squares.

"I think self-portraiture provides a notion of myself," I said carefully. "A way to observe myself and my experiences, my body and how it changes."

He walked over to the drafting table where I sliced the negatives and the enlarged prints into the pieces I used to assemble the composites. He looked over the images hanging on the line, sipped his coffee. I could feel my skin flush everywhere he looked, as though the images were part of me, as though I could feel his gaze on my skin.

"You keep this observation limited."

"Limited?"

"Something's missing. It's intentional, yes?"

I finished my coffee. "I almost never photograph my face, is that what you mean?"

He nodded. "When you do it's blurred, out of focus or in motion, your eyes closed. Why?"

I shrugged, unsure why I was being so honest. Or really, I knew why: I couldn't lie to him. Not while he was looking at my skin, my body, while he was looking over my photos. He would see it there: the truths, the lies.

"I don't know really. I don't try to solve the mysteries, only document the personal symbols or the mythologies. The shape of the space I take up." Putting down my cup I walked over to the drafting table, sorting through some photos. He stood very close to me.

"Perhaps," he said, hesitating, "this is not so different as believing your soul has been captured in the camera."

I was aware of every moment of distance between us, I could feel how desperately I wanted him to close that space. For one long painful second, I thought he would. But without awkwardness, as if by some silent cue, we instead returned to our corners.

Fed on coffee and cinnamon, I worked late into the night. Darkness fell around us until there was only my small pool of light and his larger one, the music from his portable speaker hovering softly in the vast dark space between us. I was so absorbed in the cut and fold and curl of paper, the slice of the razor and the bone folder I didn't notice him packing up for the night until he walked up behind me, ready to go with his black cargo bag slung across his chest. He leaned over my shoulder.

"You shouldn't walk up behind someone with a knife."

"I trust your focus." He said and we smiled.

"Risky."

"Its impressive, you know. You are so focused. It's good. Necessary for good art."

I shivered at the texture in his voice as it slid against my skin, and pulled myself up, spine and muscles tight. Put the knife down. Flexed my hand. It was only then I noticed my hands were sore, my fingers curled and stiff.

"This place makes it easy. All the room, the high ceilings. Ideas need space, even my small ideas."

"These are not small ideas," he said softly, pressing his fingertips into my drafting table. I looked down my sliced-up photo, a narrow diamond of my body scored and cut, empty. Beside it was a church I photographed in Paris, I was midway through cutting out its iron spire, carefully cutting around curling crosses. It was going to grow out of my chest with an airy delicacy, cut free from the sky.

He looked over my body in the photograph.

"Art is a strange thing. Especially now, when being a product is more fashionable. You have to know why you are doing it, even if no one else does. Why you will keep doing it, no matter what."

I was bound to love him for that, if nothing else. But I wasn't there yet. I was wrung out with wanting and confusion. there was a drunken glassiness to every moment we spent together. But I didn't know I loved him. I knew he was happy I was there. I could tell. Or thought I could. Sometimes he would drift toward me, a fresh cup of coffee or sparkling water in his hand. We would talk about books, the changing season, the minor tasks that took up our time.

Most days his work was repetitive, linking silver chains in strands dozens of feet long, breaking mirrors into vicious shapes by scoring and splitting the glass, covering it with tape and cracking it with a hammer. Sometimes he talked about his cat, a nameless animal, and I would smile, trying to imagine it, an artist-monk with a cat. We spoke of the cities I visited on those days I vanished from the studio. He would stand to my right, away from my working left hand, watching my knife or pearly bone folder moving silent across photo paper.

"Your cuts are so precise," he said. "And these photos, the process...they remind me of nothing else. No other work."

He walked along the wall of windows where hung the completed cutouts, where they would wait for me to paste them together. I had completed only a handful so far, but I imagined dozens of photos, large black-and-white composites, possibly a never-ending series.

"So much like themselves." He looked at me, moved closer. "You don't draw anything, do you? You don't plan them on paper first?"

"I plan them in my head I suppose. I make a test print, sometimes I'll mock it up in photoshop. Only sometimes, if it's really complex and hard to make a pattern. But not really, no, I don't draw or even measure really, not even the photo symmetry. The shape of the paper is its measurement. It is its own little set of unchanging conditions. Besides," I shrugged, "I don't see a point in writing down instructions I'm making up as I go."

He laughed, smiled at me with his canine teeth pressed together. Sharp. Whenever he did this, I felt an intensity of emotion I couldn't articulate; I had no idea what it was he might be feeling but I wanted to touch him. I did no such thing. I wanted to run my hand up his arm and across his chest.

I only nodded. Wanted.

Just because you can't see something doesn't mean it isn't there. And at any given time, there was a host of invisible things around us. Lust. Desperation. Admiration. So much want and want and want. There are clairvoyants who see ghosts, but only those saturated in lust see echoes of events that didn't happen: touching his arm, his arms around me, his teeth dragging along my thigh…. Lust haunted me, more ephemeral than any ghost. I wondered how it wasn't a red mist in the air. A dense, red fog of want, the same color as a darkroom light.

*Eat my heart out. Please. Please. Rattle my bones.*

But it felt to me as though he was curious and nothing more. Plain and simple. Curious about me. Because he liked me and maybe wasn't too sure about why.

"You know, it is good that you are here with me as I do this," he said. "It feels correct. This space, being here. I am lucky to have found you."

"We're both lucky. This is a gift, this kind of time. A space like this." I could feel a blush touch the skin of my throat.

"It's different for you, I think. This is an extra in your life, a dream, a place on the fringes of things." The way he said it, with a sense of genuine sadness, saved it from seeming like a dismissal. He wasn't looking at the photos anymore but out the window, holding a cup in one large, curled hand, speckled with white paint for a mirror frame. "But for me, this is it. This is everything. This space, what happens here is everything to me. Which is why I'm so glad you're a part of it. When I leave here, wherever this piece takes me, I'll be happy for this time."

I could have said a lot of things. I wanted to say that my real life had fewer furnishings than he assumed. There was only an empty apartment, a bed, an armchair I would read in. My camera equipment. A suitcase under the bed that could easily hold all my clothes. I wanted to say the only real mystery of my life was how someone that felt so deeply could, at the same time, contain so much emptiness. I wanted to say that I didn't understand how he could think I was anything at all.

I didn't say this to him. I only nodded, watched his profile, the glimmer of his copper eyes in the dusk. I wanted to step forward, closer, touch him in the way I wanted him to touch me, but I still didn't know how. When I did speak, the words came out in knots, in a stranger's voice.

"The common thread throughout my life is that I feel things no one else does. Maybe my imagination. It never translates fully into the world, like it is somehow less in reality. Like asking other people to understand it reduces it somehow? This room is the only place where that's not true."

He smiled and then took my hand, squeezed my it, looked down at the tangle of our fingers together, and then back out the skyline, purple with evening.

"The world doesn't have that kind of power." He said softly, almost to himself. "Nothing could ever make you less real."

It could have been pretension or arrogance. It could have been dripping in invisible misogyny; it could have been a lot of things. But it wasn't. It was just what he thought, stated in a casually powerful way, with authority. Said like wind: empty but for the force of its gale.

Before I slept that night, I let myself jump off wild black cliffs of my imagination and found his voice pouring over me, the sound of him working behind me, erotic and tender. The sound of him was a fixation. I did not need to fantasize, imagine him touching me with his hands or his mouth, only his voice's graveled texture in a near whisper, the dark arch as it grew in volume and detail. I did not think about the feel of him, chest and arms and deep pounding breaths as he hugged me, or the time his hand touched mine across the small table as we took our tea. I thought only about my hands, sliding down my stomach, my sex, cupped around my wetness.

Slowly, stroking, feeling every intense rush of blood, the swell of nerves and flesh, I smiled, could feel myself smiling as my fingers slipped inside, palm glancing softly across my clit as sensations echoed down, where my curling fingers spread. My pleasure was passive, floating, so it felt as though only his naked voice touched me. I could feel my sex flutter like a petal at each half-unconscious curl of my fingers and then, the sudden tautness around my fingers as I came, a milky sensation expanding over my skin.

His voice riding out of me with a sigh.


I spent all the next afternoon in the darkroom, developing a few rolls of street photography and a portrait session, feeling at home in the dark with the smooth, clean, astringent smell of the developer fluid, my hands working by muscle memory.

We had both been there for hours working silently in our own spaces, as though we were an organic part of it, as much a part of it as the massive windows and rolling doors, like the moss growing on the walls, the empty hallways.

When I came out of the darkroom, blinking into the

brightness of the afternoon light, all the windows were wide open. The massive space was full of moving air and the faint scent of soldering wire. He was turning, before my eyes, a pile of shattered glass and mirrors into a massive frozen moment of an explosion. I stood watching, and as my eyes adjusted to the brightness, the shine from the mirror and glass edges and dust did not diminish.

"It's beautiful," I said, surprised how my voice echoed.

He stopped working, put down the soldering gun and looked at me. After a while he stepped down off the step ladder.

"You have never said that word before, I don't think."

"Oh?"

"Beautiful," he said. "I've never heard you say it."

I looked up at him, the light through the window shone on him like a halo and I looked away. It was like he folded my heart up into a little origami star, sharp points, bright. I wondered how to explain.

"Beautiful is a word I try not to use."

Leaving his soldering iron to cool, the windows still open, he put water in the kettle and placed it on the hotplate.

"Why, exactly?"

"It's personal. I guess maybe it's hard to explain."

"Try."

I didn't say anything for a long time. I walked around the metal frame of the sculpture, shards of glass clinging to it like frost. He only watched, made coffee, seemed to know I was thinking. I took my time, trying to fold words around the feeling, like mirrors folded around his metal frame. How to say what I felt without giving myself away.

"What we find beautiful says so much about us. So, I try not to use it because what I find beautiful reveals a lot about who I am."

"What do you mean?" he asked.

"A true image, a true moment or a true thing is made of light and darkness, the harmony and tension between them. I think beauty lives inside that tension." I watched him stir together coffee and boiling water, watched him watch the coffee steep into our cups, I paid careful attention to the way his body moved under his clothes.

"And what do you find beautiful?"

"Sensation. The places between myself and oblivion, the chaos of overstimulation." I hesitated. "Sometimes that means pain."

The words in my mouth tasted like the wilderness, a wild wet stone, sharp grass, river water and dirt. He nodded, sipped his coffee from a jadeite mug. Setting down one of the pale green cups beside me, he moved to my photos, as he had before looked over them, hanging behind a row of fresh film, waiting to be cut.

"I can see it in your photos. Do you try to show it there?"

"For a long time, I wanted things without knowing I wanted them," I said, sitting in the half collapsed armchair, curled up like a cat, and I didn't know how I got there, how I was saying what I was about to say. It was like I just woke up mid-sentence, about to tell a secret, or perhaps already told one.

Already said too much.

No escape.

"Like mapping dark matter. Even before I knew what beauty really was." I was unable to watch him listening to me, because he was listening very intently. I looked out the windows, watching the clouds crawling across the sky in lace tatters. "There is a sincerity in those places, a kind of undeniable experience of the self. Maybe some of my photos express it, the way I want it, or what I want beauty to feel like. Maybe a handful of photographs that I've taken really show it."

He moved closer to me as I spoke, the space between us vibrating with how quickly he closed it, how much of it there still was. He reached down, his hand closed around my arm. Closing hard, viperous quick.

Little pools of pain opened under his fingertips, pressing hollows into my skin. The pain, the close press of him, looming. I stood, drawn by the focus in his eyes, a seriousness that demanded my attention. His voice was a coiled snarl, dark velvet when he spoke. It didn't sound tender or promising. It sounded like a warning: you will regret this.

"I can show you oblivion."

He kissed me then, sudden and brutal. His mouth was vicious, the kiss a long deep attack directly on my heart. When we pulled away, gasping, my mouth hurt, my entire body was lit up, shining. He held me, hands hard, hurting me, holding my body close to him.

"I know what you want. In essence, if not in particular.

I recognized it in you immediately." His jaw clenched. "And when you showed me your work, it was right there."

Relief and tension in a tightly braided cord tied us together. Tied kiss to lip. Skin to bone. Hands to body. His hands dug hard into my arms, my hair, my throat, pulling me toward him, crushing me. It felt like a gift, and I shivered. He kissed me again, hands digging into me so hard I whimpered into his mouth. I was terrified, trying to believe it was happening, trying to memorize every moment, every atom of him.

*Hard, please. Harder.* I wanted to say, but I only kissed him back, desperate almost immediately. I looked at him, and he looked back serenely. He knew he had me.

"I want to do horrible things to you."

His voice was a snarl, a surrender. And all I could do was nod my consent. I knew everything. Every moment waiting for us. Some profound stirring confirmation of fate or chemistry. A huge, deep swoop of his arms lifted me from the floor and enclosed me in darkness. He smelled like devastation, like witchcraft. Wormwood, nightshade, tobacco, cinnamon, the sharp tang of silver from his soldering gun, metal smoke like blood. He smelled like all the danger that can exist just after dusk.

But I was no corrupted female saint, no virgin taken by the dark. I had no ice to crack, no virgin hesitation to conquer, no heightened value of resistance or purity. I was open, ready, one with my want which was kindled and burning in the deepest parts of myself. Such a thing: to burn and be seen.

His eyes were copper in the falling evening around us,

red like an Egyptian drawing of a setting sun. When he kissed me again, the sharp of his teeth bit the soft of my lower lip, hard, harder as though trying to devour me. I tasted blood, a red edge to his kiss, and my mouth watered, open, wanting.

His massive hand closed around my throat, his arm extending out. I knew everything I needed to know about him as the world filled with static. I knew he could shatter reality, toss me out in churning water filled with blue electric sound. I knew he could lead me back to living, the close embrace of darkness and light.

Slowly, he undressed me. Lifted my T-shirt and slid my jeans down my legs. He looked at me from every angle, a brightness in his eyes. He picked up a knife from my worktable and traced it slow against my skin, cut my bra's straps, the hips of my underwear. Even though his movements were slow, they vibrated with heavy energy. Speed, violence, just a moment away from my skin. Careful, so careful, allowing only the barest pass of cold as the edge slid against me.

It is impossible to let someone hold a knife to you and not think of your own death, and at that moment, I could have died of happiness.

He let the pieces fall in tangles and tatters on my bare feet. Only when I was utterly naked did he touch me. His fingers brushing over the small bottom-weight of my breasts, the plush tender points of my nipples, which puckered at his touch. He touched me with his hands and his eyes, stood close and touched me with his breath.

"I want to hit you."

His voice was rough and ragged. His hands flexed, calloused from work, the sleeves of his shirt rolled up over his forearms, thick with jumping muscles under tattooed skin. The expression on his face was chilling, cold. A hard-set stare, violent, vicious but barely contained.

"Will it hurt?" I asked.

"It will." He nodded once, eyes on mine. "It will hurt. I will hurt you. First there will be pain, and then, it will be warm. If I hit you hard enough your skin will feel roasted. Hot. Swollen."

His hand cupped my cheek gently, his other hand touched my hip, my ass, slid farther down between my legs. I suppressed a moan and he smiled because he found I was wet. My body understood everything he said was both a warning and a seduction. A single hard breath escaped me as I tried to keep myself together.

"You are warm, burning already. Is this for me?"

I nodded and he responded with a sigh, a sly, vicious smile, his voice full of gravel as he spoke.

"Do you want me to hit you?"

"Yes. Please."

He kissed me again, long breaths, long kisses. The language of want is spoken in breaths. I nodded, closed my eyes as he pressed his hand more firmly against my sex. My body responded automatically. I sighed against my will, bowed my head. No shame. Reverence. He continued to stroke between my legs.

*Do whatever you want to me.* I wanted to say but something kept the words tied inside me. It was dangerous to say that to this man. I realized I had met my match, a man I believed, easily and honestly believed, wanted the same things I did—but more. More vicious, more ready.

*Hurt me. Hurt me.* I thought as his hand slid over the swell of my ass, my breasts, his touch rough, like sandpaper. Pulling hard on a nipple, a small spike of pain.

*Finally.*

"I want to make you bright." His voice was rough as his touch. "I want to make you shine."

He pulled his hands away, and I almost fell forward, following their vanishing motion. I did not let myself moan, but I wanted to. Even the sudden clench of absence made me quake in pleasure. My hands opened and closed. It was tempting, so tempting, to think I could reach down, caress myself and come in a moment, under his gaze. It was amazing to think that maybe he wouldn't let me.

I stood there, for a long moment under his gaze, warm and ready for his touch. I did not move. I only stood, breathing, pulsing with want. He smiled and suddenly was very close to me again, one hand on my face, brushing my hair away out of my eyes, tracing the edge of my shoulder. His other hand fell, closed on the slip of my waist. I watched his eyes moving around my face, my mouth, my eyes. My mouth again. Lingering.

"If you say yes, if you give yourself to me, I will hurt you, I...I will make you cry. I will mark your skin, if you let me."

His fist closed in my hair, harder. Harder. He tugged my head back with a slow steady motion, drew me up onto my toes, his other hand closing slow and tight around my throat. My hands moved to his wrist, holding him there, trying not to pull him away.

"I want to leave marks on your skin. I want to beat the breath out of you. I want to…take care of you."

His touch was gentle again, his voice soft, heavy with want. He loosened his grip, but kept his hands on me, kept me pressed against him, held. He gave up his voice, breath escaping. Every word was true. He was hard; I could feel it. And the idea of his cock hard against my body made my head spin. His words were too true. I almost didn't know how to hear them. Knowing he wanted me made my throat dry. I could only nod my head. He held me up, pressed his forehead against mine, bowing over me, his breath deep. Growing steady.

I was massively aware of my nakedness against his clothes, his bare arms brushing my back. I almost moaned. He looked down at me with a steady gaze, a slow unbelieving breath, so much like awe. it made everything inside me clench.

"I have never—never—wanted someone like this. Approached someone like this. But you are…Please, let me touch you…"

He shook his head, looking down at me. A breath escaped him, a laugh that was almost bitter, angry. He searched my face, copper eyes focused, dark, conflicted. The measuring eyes of a cautious animal who has survived many traps.

"Your eyes get darker when you're aroused. Did you know that?"

"No," I said.

"Are you sure about this?"

I did not move other than to nod my consent. When I spoke, the voice sounded more familiar, more like my own. "I am sure. Yes. Please, yes."

I saw him raise his hand. Fear fluttered in my face like a moth, obscuring my vision, but I lifted my chin with the impact flashed, passed. A single ring of sound clapped around my head, bracketed by silence. A cold, brutal wave of sting rocking down my body.

Too close. Too close. And brutal.

A wave of arousal moved through me. His palm pressed against my cheek, absorbing the shock, spreading it out. I did moan then, a shocking sound. Even though I asked for it, the slap was a hard unsettling shock, pain full of a close sense invasion of it. He sighed and stepped away.

"This too much, too soon. We are moving too quickly." He kissed me hard. Hands in my hair, my skin stinging, my cheek bright with static. "Lust will drag us around if we are not careful. We need to be more careful."

"I know what I want."

"We have lots of time…"

I nodded, confirming that I knew he was right and that he could drag me around. I was so naked. It would be wrong to lay myself out, offer myself up, in the first wave of possibility. It would be wrong to rush.

But part of me did not care. The part that felt the weight of my breasts against his chest, that shivered at his touch. The parts of me that quivered at his words, knew how naked I was next to him, fully dressed, still in his boots, and loved it—didn't care. But the rational part of my mind told me the truth. It was real. Sudden and almost impossible, and against all odds, but real. And I needed to decide this when I wasn't drunk on lust. Dressed. I wondered if I had been sober at all in the last few weeks, working beside him, drinking him in.

"I will drive you home."

# 4.

In his small black car, driving east toward my apartment, he kissed me at a red light. His hand grasping hard, buried between my legs, the car flooded with red light. Deep and vicious. And all the kisses that had not yet been given hung over our heads like a sword. Offering promise. And its other edge: pain. Everything luscious. He took my hand and a moment later turned down a side street. Winchester Lane.

"I'm a patient man," he said, "but I am only human."

And even then, with a kiss that could only be human, I didn't quite believe him. I was ensnared by an animal or fate. In that moment, I learned what dangerous meant. Not only something that could hurt me, with his fist gripping the rail of my wrist, tangled in my hair. It meant something else too, something that felt safe, that was safe, but promised still to tear and bite and feed.

Something beautiful and violent.

It occurred to me, not for the first time, that this world we made was not so different from the worlds I imagined for my photos and his installations. A portion of reality we made ours. His. Mine. I was happy to be in our hidden lair, more than satisfied; I was honored. I could no more refuse him than a shore refuses the tide, a moon its orbit. His hands were massive, and after, for days after, everywhere I went, he was with me.

"I am going to hit you again."

I could only nod. Keeping hold of me, he used the hand

that had been fondling me to slap me again, close and brutal and still not hard. I gasped at the suddenness of it, the brightness of the static sparking across my cheekbone. Not pain, not yet, only brightness. I did not wonder what I did to deserve or earn it. I did nothing or everything; it didn't matter. There was only his want and mine, equally matched. I opened my eyes, looked at him, his eyes dark, almost black, looking at the place he'd hit me, which buzzed, still glowing. He touched my cheek gently.

"Do you trust me?" he asked, pulling away, my skin crying out for his hands again, but they curled into fists. I knew he wanted to touch me, to hit me again, but instead, he put his hands on the wheel.

"I think so." Trust him. I wanted to kneel at his feet.


I didn't tell Ruby about the neat rows of bruises on my arms from the grip of his hands, but we talked almost endlessly about that night. Or, at least, the parts I told her, carefully. We'd had been friends since a writing course we took a few years before. She went back to school full time, first as a graduate student in literature, then working for a fellowship. When I met her for coffee in her apartment the day after he drove me home, I could still feel him all over me. I had to tell her, in part, because I knew she would read it all over me anyway, even if she never saw the little purple starburst on my arm.

She rubbed my shoulders, cleaned away a stack of books and notebooks, and poured us wine even though it was early.

"I have never wanted anything," I said, "nothing the way I want this. But I don't know if I should trust it."

"Do you need to ask? Men will be men will be men."

I shook my head. It hurt.

"That isn't it. It's not so simple. It can't be. I want him, I just can't figure out what he wants with me. Me specifically."

"What do you mean?"

"In the right room, he's basically famous. His work is in museums. I'm a tech for auction houses."

"Bullshit. You know as well as I do those men aren't magic, and they seldom deserve their places. And you, well. You're beautiful, and your photos are incredible and beautiful. He'd be mad not to want you. Maybe it is just his way, to be all mysterious."

"It doesn't feel like his 'way', like fake mysterious. It feels like, more than that, somehow. It feels...fundamental? Biological? I don't know. There's a way of talking—of looking—like he is reflecting me, really seeing me."

"You're saying he has the seducer's eyes. He sounds like a tricky spider."

"No. It's much more transparent than seduction. He's not trying to impress me; it's like he's trying to talk me out of it."

She laughed, and I wondered if she knew how literal I was being.

"Babe, all I know is, one moment he wasn't there, and the next he was. You should be careful."

She was correct; I did need to be careful. He was a

shining and sudden dark light, but I could not summon a sense this was wrong, sinister. Ruby looked at me for a long time, straight in the eyes.

"I know."

"And look. If he's trying to warn you off, maybe you should listen."

I nodded, but I knew, even as I feared the worst, suspected it, I was going to do it. I was going to trust him. At the thought of him, my heart folded in an intricate origami of want. People talk about their heart skipping a beat, but that is not what happened. The thought of him, the involuntary sense memory of the taste of his mouth, the grip of his hands, the smell of him like wrath and blood and smoke and metal, would make my heart fold and unfold in all its vivid vascular detail. Beautiful and shivering in pleasure. My heart could feel pleasure, as though it had been touched. What a thing to learn about your body.

I arrived at the studio, heart pounding, nervousness closing around me as I climbed the stairs, my vision puddled into blue light. I moved toward him carefully, closing the space, my body pounding with trepidation. Fear, real fear, trembling, tumbling around inside me with desire. He was standing by the over-stuffed chairs, waiting. Arms crossed.

I slid the door closed behind me with a hard bang. The sound of it made my hands tingle. My blood screamed. And he began by slowly moving toward me, an easy walk, a predator's prowl. I took a step forward and he held up his hand calmly, with no effort. I stopped. Stood still. My hands at my sides, tingling.

He undressed me again. The same careful touch, the brush of fabric against my skin. As he cut away the straps of my bra and underwear, with satisfying crunching fabric sounds, he let me feel the edge of the blade as it slid against my skin, cold and sharp. Almost pressing, so I would feel it shiver across my skin but not cut me.

He claimed the topography of my body by sliding the blade slow and easy over me. I was still as death, careful even to breathe against the point he pressed into my throat, the bottom-heavy swell of my breasts. The knife slipped over the dip of waist and hip, around the little swell of my stomach below my belly button. The blade pressed into my inner thigh.

*He could slip that knife inside me before I could even know to stop him.* The thought was sudden and full of fear, clear and sharp as a bell in sunlight. A red line. The knife traced, pressed and dragged, leaving long white lines. Reaching up with the knife, he cut the elastic band holding my hair back with a slow slick slide of the blade, gentle as anything. And only then did he touch me, capturing my mouth in a savage kiss, sharp as though to wound me. My heart broke with fear, a kiss as dangerous as a knife.

It is impossible to let someone hold a knife to you, to press and press, to leave red marks like a comet across the sky, to feel the vault of your blood just below, just inside, just on the other side of that silver shine, and not consider for a moment your own death.

The shreds of my clothes fell around my feet as if they were made of paper. I stood, naked except for the weight of his gaze. He traced the knife over my skin, down my arms, across my chest. Pressed, lightly, just lightly, against the inside of my thigh. Press and drag, leaving a white scratch over the swell of my thigh. The knife vanished, and he reached up with empty hands and loosened my hair, down my shoulders.

I pressed myself into him, feeling the fabric of his shirt, the brush of his jeans, his forearms and rough hands slid over my body. He kissed me almost constantly, hands over my breasts, the painful weight of them pressing so hard on my skin, red marks bloomed around his fingers like halos.

My hunger rose quickly, like madness, blinding, urgent. But he ignored my movements of impatience and want. His hands traced over my skin, pressed deeply into me.

Gently, he took me by the shoulders, guided me to the center of the studio under a silver hoop now hanging from a rafter at the end of one of his long black ropes. Silently, he wrapped my arms and shoulders in rope, coiled it around my ribs and chest locking off the rope around my arms. The rope held me impossibly still, taut against me as I breathed.

He moved the rope with constant steady pressure, perfectly even against every inch of skin, like the finely muscled body of a snake. He looped this harness to the hoop shining over my head like a halo and pulled it taut with a clean direct motion. In all that time, we didn't say a word to each other. We spoke through movement and glances, the pressure of touch. I closed my eyes, felt the vibrating tension of an object in use, the focus of intent and expertise.

When he was done, I was almost standing on my toes but still balanced. My hips and pelvis lifted high over my legs. The backward, downward tie of my arms lifted my breasts, thrust them up, filling me with a sense of how tender, how hurtable they were. I was, at that moment—his. I concentrated on my breathing, my balance. Stepping back, he surveyed me, then he sat in the armchair and continued sipping his coffee.

"I was right," he said with a satisfied tone in voice, an easy sigh, "you like this."

The questions he asked were clinical, personal but asked with careful civility. He asked about my work schedule and time obligations, my sexual experience and how I would describe my orientation, desires, limitations, fears, everything in minute detail. It was hard to remember to breathe, find my voice, to keep looking at him. I was warm and flush with summer light and heat, so slick with sweat under the rope. But I had to fight to keep from trembling.

And then he stood, closed the distance between us. I thought he would touch me, but he took out a measuring tape and recorded my height, waist, my wrists and the width of my throat, lifting my hair gently out of the way. I tried to take steady breaths.

Finally, he touched me, keeping one hand over my heart. He moved his other hand down to my sex, where he opened his hand gently, smiling his approval to find me wet.

And then he stepped away, my body bowed out to him, pleading. And he turned back, slammed his hand into my chest, so my breath skipped out in a cough. His hand was so wide it gripped my entire chest in its span, curled around the ropes and squeezed. I could feel rope everywhere, wake up and groan, and tremble.

"Do you remember what I said to you before you left?"

I nodded as best I could, breathing into the pain that cut into my skin, all rope around my body pulled toward him.

"I want you warmer."

He repeated it, and I moaned, unable to stop myself, my body so exposed, so open, so beyond my control.

"More hot and wet than you can stand."

I did not move. I listened to his hand rise and fall; a single sound bracketed by silence. A hot slap, a brutal wave of sting rolled up my body, his palm pressed hard, absorbing the shock, spreading it out.

"I want you to hurt."

The hand that caressed was smooth now, soft like his voice.

"Until you cannot stand anymore, cannot bear another second."

He struck again, and I willed myself not to move. He struck again, harder. Stars danced across my skin with the heat he called up under my skin with his voice and his hands. Burning bright. Again, the hardest yet. I gasped, whimpered, cowered inside the harness that held me. The rope was a comfort even though it would not let me escape, offering restraint against my desire to tremble.

"Count Five. Or say thank you."

"Five," I said with a sob. Leaning over, he gave me one long kiss. Struck me again.

"Six." His voice was hard, cruel. It was an order. "Or say thank you."

I took long breaths.

"Answer me."

Again, I counted, contracted in pain.

"Six" The slap rolled up my body, so even my scalp was crawling. Something like impact, something like grace. My skin and everything miles deeper began to hurt. And sing.

"Seven."

"Breathe," he said tenderly and hit me again. Harder. I cried out. An animal sound rolled out of me with the sensations as I took a breath.

"Another breath."

I took another long deep breath.

"Good girl."

Breathing out steady, like a sigh. Again and again, he hit me the exhales. My voice cracking as I counted. Single words braced with waiting for the strike to fall, the wait…

He reached down and touched me. His hand was hot from hitting me, rounding over the pink of my ass. He rested his hand there for a moment on the rough moss of pain on my skin. After a moment, he moved away and I stayed very still, listening to him move around me. My skin was humming, singing, waiting for him to touch me again.

And then he was behind me, arms around me, cupping my breasts. He kissed my shoulder; every movement pressed us closer together. He bit my shoulder with a snarl deep in his mouth. He bit the back of my neck, gripped the rope hard. He bit down harder, and fresh tears came to my eyes. Pain blossomed under his teeth, bloomed like a flower.

Curling an arm around me, he released the rope securing me to the hoop, and the gentle, tight pressure encircling me vanished, still held immobile by the harness, my legs folded, and I fell, fell...against him. His arms holding me as we both folded onto the floor. He unwound the rope, moving it away from my body with the same slow even pressure with which he laid it on. It amazed me even in my haze.

He freed me from the rope, curled up behind me so I was resting against him with gentle touches of his hands, running fingers lightly over the red bites of rope tracing into the curves of my arms and wrists.

"Are you alright?" He asked, a whisper as gentle as his touch.

"I'm wonderful." I nodded, kneeling up and turning to look at him, leaning forward with my head pressed against his. He kissed me softly and then lay me down, a press against the back of my neck to push me to the floor.

"Stay."

Standing, he walked back to the chairs, stripped off his clothes slowly. His body was cut in large proportion. Wide back and massive chest, long arms. His cock was heavy, firm. He sat down and gestured to me, letting me crawl forward, and I did, my arms trembling from the tie, marked with spirals.

At his direction, I took his cock into my mouth, gently at first, my tongue sliding around the thickness of his head, the flared edge. And then, deeper. I opened my jaw wide to pull him as deep as I could before his width filled my mouth. Drool poured from my lips, slicked my hands as I ran them over his shaft where my mouth and throat could not reach.

He pulled me up, saliva dripping from my chin. He kissed me, bit my mouth, my nipples, the weight at the bottom of my breasts. He threw me to the floor and knelt above me, fell on me, kissed and bit my belly, my thighs with hard, snarling bites. Leaving cold rings of pain, I knew would bloom into purple bruises. Great mouthfuls of flesh vanished behind his teeth, and I imagined his mouth returning bloody, his lips dripping. I was devoured, like a ripe fruit still hanging on the tree. Devoured.

His hands went everywhere, in my hair, my sex, my mouth. There was no part of my body I could hide from him. No detail I wanted to. His touch was violent, tender, too soft, too hard. His cock brushed against my thigh, my ass. My body, my mind, every part of me was painfully awake, aware and sensitive. With his hands, he ground me down deeply into me. Pain wafting off my skin, out of my hair like smoke. My body was slick with sweat.

Kneeling over me, he lifted my pelvis to raise me to him. My body quaking crisscrossed red marks from his touch, his teeth, the rough press of his rope. Honey was pouring from me, slick between my thighs. And shockingly, suddenly, he pushed his cock into me, the swollen pulsing walls of my cunt screaming in pain and relief. The size of him spreading me open.

All the air was drawn from me, the way his cock filled

me, touching the tip of my sex with each thrust of his body, but as soon as my breathing hastened and my sex clenched hungrily, he would draw out, glistening, and take up another rhythm. He pressed me down into the floor, holding my legs apart, forcing himself up to the hilt; he hauled me up onto my knees and fucked me hard, reached out and clenched a fist in my hair. He spun me on my back and pressed me into the floor, holding me down, my throat in his massive hand as he slapped me hard, closed his hand over my mouth to stifle my animal sounds.

Everything he did was reflected in his breath, the drop and darkening of his eyes. A dark hard snarling in his chest. Eventually, he was gripping me, forcing my movements so I could not come. So, I could not give in to the brutal rushing inevitable.

"Not yet." His voice was ragged, cut with a hard growl. A demand I heard in the haze of pain and exaltation, and I begged my sobbing body to obey.

"Not yet." Caught in this avalanche of sensation, pleasure, I lost all orientation on my body in space and time. He fucked the way he spoke. Hard, with an authority that wasn't so much implied as intrinsic. My hair fell down my back, his hands dug hard and deep into the curve of my hips, his body slamming into mine, holding me in place with the vicious grip.

"Now," he said. An order, and my body, trembling on the edge of darkness, and ready, so ready, fell into the black. Obeyed. I came, feeling the walls of my cunt clenching down around him in a long span of rapid waves, a rapid fluttering inside me, like the valves of a heart opening and closing.

And in an elusive and rare moment that to so many lovers looks like fate, I felt the deep thrum and pulse of his cock, timed with a brutal snarl from his chest and a glowing growl as he came with me. We came together, hard, with one voice, and he collapsed over me, chest pressed into my back. Again, his teeth found the back of my neck and dug deep. Hard. I whimpered, my throat sore from gasping, my heart full of light. So full it felt like light would shine out of my mouth.

I sobbed.

My orgasm broke the wave of tension that began with pain, the adrenalin of agony. My skin thrummed with my pulse, with love and joy like nothing I had ever known. He was smiling softly, panting as he curled around me, our skin slick with sweat. He held me on the knotted rug, the silver hoop over us like the moon. He kissed my forehead, my shoulders, licked my tears from my cheeks.

"Are you alright?"

I nodded, gasping, smiling. His curled fingers brushed gently up and down my arm.

"That was a lot, I know. But you are amazing."

I took a broken breath and searched myself, and smiled. I was not a tangle of static, or regret and remorse, or questions. I was myself. Inside me bloomed a room of clean white peace. And calm. Tears rolled down my face.

"I am more than alright." Trembling, awake and for a moment, this moment, aware of all my edges, my boundaries. Shockingly beautiful. I was bright, shining.

Light spilling from my body with tears, sensations echoing inside me. "I'm thrilled."

Morning lifted out of the city like a woman rising from a bath. I slipped out of bed, skin still tender from where he touched me, and pulled on my kimono. I took my clothes off the line, made coffee, and somewhere church bells rang. The olive tree cast strange shadows across the garden, forked and twisted full of singing birds.

Without warning, a memory of him washed over me. A simple nothing moment. One of the first nights we spent together, sitting side by side in the studio, right after he brought in the armchairs. We didn't touch. He wasn't even looking at me. We talked about books.

Memories appeared without warning all day. Again, and again. All my life, I wanted to touch everything inside me. Every banner of flesh. I always knew I was different, and everything around me warned me away, told me it was fury and madness, blood, abuse, not exaltation. Not romance. Certainly not love. I kept this part of myself secret. A shadow.

Pain is like desire. It has no language of its own. It must recruit metaphors and similes: knifelike, killing, burning. Sharp, dull, heavy, electric. The experience felt just beyond my grasp at every moment. Elusive as smoke. But I was learning quickly that pain was a landscape mostly bereft of words. A fusion of sensation, emotion, nerve, and memory. Irreducible. This is always true of pain, a lesson I learn again and again...

Pain is always subjective. You can never lose the "I" from it, it fuses mind and body while splitting them apart. In pain we enter a dialogue with ourselves; consciousness becomes a twin of subject and object, joined at the spot where we hurt. It turns us into observers, explorers of a natural disaster.

But what was I doing in the wilderness in the first place?

I am a masochist, and I have been for as long as I can remember. My first crushes, first fantasies, first glimpses of romantic and sexual promise were laced with shades of pain and violence. As I grew up, these desires grew with me. My innate expressions of romantic love and sexual desire are felt through the metaphors of pain and force, and physical intensity. I know now, after a long time, that masochism and power dynamics can be a healthy metaphor for love, a method or philosophy for structuring romantic and sexual experiences. But the reality of human relationships isn't simple, and that's especially true for masochists.

Complexity is insidious when you define something through its opposite. Words are fascinating in part because they capture moments that shape the self. Either their presence or their absence shapes everything we see and feel. Life is full of things that defy language, full of moments that transform, turning points, cliffs and edges. Sometimes they change who you are, and sometimes they ground you deeper in yourself—like his hands on my skin.

Transformative moments can't be anticipated; even when you knowingly answer a message, walk into the cafe, lean in for the goodnight kiss, you can't possibly know what it will be. You can't anticipate a transformation, in principle and by definition. It is impossible to know. You can only discover.

It was painful to starve desire, to second-guess instinct. For so long, I misunderstood what strength was. I believed I was strong enough to accept a flawed premise. I thought I could move through the world with desire locked up and never feel it, never feed it.

But I know now that is the life for cowards and there is a kind of hubris in thinking you can banish and starve your most vibrant self simply because you don't want to make a scene. Pain showed me that, he showed me.

I ate a pastry for breakfast, baked fresh bread. I felt loved and cared for as a nebula of bruises began to bloom on my skin.

I wanted to give him my limbs, my eyes, my skin.

My heart was naked, and I gave that to him as well.


By the time summer began to sink around us with humidity and the electric song of cicadas, I had a row of five, or so, half-compiled photos hanging off a string along my end of the studio. A stack of several more weighed down to lay flat, or polished and complete all slid into the tall stacks of the paper cabinet. Black and white photos of my body with many arms and hands, reaching to grab thighs in nylons, grip stiff posture collars, tug at my hair. My body posed and sliced and intersected with architecture, bridges, spires and skyscrapers.

One day he strung up fairy lights, and that night he

turned them on, so the massive windows glittered. Little magic lights illuminating our conversations, the fall of our bodies as we tangled around each other, fucked and moaned into the night under our Muse: Joy. I'd wait long days, long afternoons for the fall and slip of his hands. Pain, pleasure.

On the streetcar on the way to the studio, alone in the morning, I would shiver at the memory of his voice, the feeling of his hand shaped like a spear, entering me with slow deliberation. I would sit alone on airplanes on the way to shoot new collections and clench around the memory of his cock, his fist, his mouth, his voice. Once, on the way back to the city on an empty train from the airport, I almost made myself come thinking about his hands and brushing my hands gently over my nipples through my thin summer dress.

I lived in a constant steady state of arousal. My photos became more and more inspired by us, by the fever of desire I lived with. I'd shoot during golden hour, casting my shadow long against my walls, turning on my air conditioner and shooting the goosebumps. I decorated my skin with gemstone stickers, made starburst patterns around the bruises and teeth marks he left on me. Beautiful grounding memories blooming on my skin. I learned the complexity of lighting bruises, the difficulty in capturing the many layers and colors, like trying to photograph clouds.

Again and again, we crashed into each other with all the grace of lust and violence. Even saturated in lust, my time with him was kept a secret from the rest of my life, held insular and separate. Those afternoons when I'd slip away to the studio in the last blasts of summer, the sky bleached by heat, space air-conditioned against the darkening heat outdoors, and in the bright soft of summer, our nights were red and black secrets. I would look over my shoulder at the span of his body pounding into me, the roll of my hip shiny with sweat. Part of the wonder of our time was this secrecy, our insular orbit.

Some nights I went from my home to the studio at his order. Not to work, not to develop film. One such night I entered the studio to find a bed waiting for me. A white iron frame standing in the center between our spaces, taking up some of the areas where we would take our coffee, pressing the armchairs closer together.

The bed was facing the row of windows, so no part the ample surface of rumpled duvets and pillows was hidden from the light spilling in. It was beautiful, a perfectly white cloud of linen to make me a violated Sleeping Beauty, pricked and bled and beaten by something wicked, into submission, into sleep. Between the bed and the door, he stood with a cane in his hand.

Desire lies on the other side of fear.

I dropped to my knees. A familiar motion now as he pulled off my sundress, grabbed my hair and tilted my head back. He pressed the cane against my lips until I opened my mouth for it. He walked with me, fist still in my hair as I crawled to bed. The idea of the cane made me tremble and I tried not to drool as I carried it in my mouth. At the bed's white billowing horizon, he took the cane from me.

"Stand."

He removed my bra, unhooking it from the front, pulling my underwear down from around my waist. He stuffed them in my mouth so I could smell their soapy smell, the scent of my skin, faintly of my sex. I stood, and he reached out to touch me, his hand falling down my spine to the small of my back. He stood taller. We both did.

And then it was happening.

Did I say I was ready? I wasn't.

It is impossible to be ready, really. He was kind at first, tapping gently around the swell of my ass, bringing up a slow warmth. He struck me once, hard, a quick snap. A shock, an invasion, a readjustment of everything, including—especially perhaps—my will. Myself. My heart and skin.

You can never actually be ready for a hard stroke of a cane.

It sparks and burns white-hot. It roars in crystal, sharp and blunt at once. He struck me again. And again. Every stroke was a long experience of pain. A rapid sunrise, light moving through my skin. Five hard strokes, one after the other, each one a little harder. Harder.

I cried.

When he let me, I slid to my knees against the bed, and he held out the cane for me to kiss. I kissed his hands. He kissed me softly. A little bit of life pressed against my mouth.

I was slick with sweat, my entire body warm like I was running a fever. He stroked the back of my head, wiped my tears and then gathered me up and put me in the bed. The sheets were cool, heavy like watercolor paper, they felt stiff against my marked skin. He slid a collar around my throat and chained me to the headboard. In the endless white of the bed, chain rattling, he fucked me hard and fast on all fours. At first, there was only the pain of the marks and depth and the rhythm. But soon, I begin to feel the little pleasures, the sweetness of his belly and the muscles across his pelvis and the tops of his thighs brushing against painful welts from the cane on my ass, the way his hands gripped into me. He took his time, fucking hard, steady, luxuriously pressing me into the bed so he was all I could feel, floating, buffeted by waves of sensation.

I hardly made a sound.

Afterward, he unhooked the chain, and I bowed my head, thanking him. He kissed me, softly, a gentle touch to my face, and buried us both beneath the covers of the unmade bed, stained and rumpled, sheets pulled into standing peaks, like the surface of the ocean.


The cane marks were angry. Dark purple, almost plum. Velvet in texture and shot through their centers with vivid white welts. They hurt, stung in the bath, ached when I sat down, tugged as I moved through a yoga sequence. I loved them, I felt solid and quiet. healthy and vibrant. I wondered if this contained feeling was what one would call being centered. I photographed the marks in natural evening light, tender moody bruises resembling rough sunsets, swollen like storm clouds.

I would wake in the morning from a deep sleep and move and stretch and find all the places on my body glowing softly with fresh bruises, small swollen welts, the promise of future wounds, the dull of pulled and stretched and tired muscles. I would map his body to mine in the shower by the marks we left behind: Bite marks on my thighs like dark velvet butterfly wings, his fingerprints in a blue-purple ink of blood under my skin.

Desire and want are strange and elastic entities. The body knows what it wants, even if we do not, even if it is dangerous. When I was with him, the air moved between us. Time passed more slowly. Words and gestures deepened, meant more. I would slide the studio door closed and bolt the lock behind me, and we wouldn't say a word. It would be silent before he pulled me against him. A hard embrace that pressed my body close to his.

When we did speak, sometimes with him still holding me very close, I would be able to feel his voice hum in his chest. It became a ritual. Taking softly together, our bodies close and sick from sweat after fucking. A lot of rituals grew between us; the way I kissed the cane or a strap, his belt or his hands, the way he handed me a cup of coffee, the way I would strip off my clothes at the door and crawl naked to our bed, kneel beside it with my thighs open to him, my mouth parted, palms up.

Sometimes, after greeting me, breathing in the smell of me, feeling my body against him, he would ignore me. Sometimes he would tell me to go work. Other times he would leave me kneeling by the bed and move around the studio, music and the sound of work filling the room. Sometimes I would have to wait a long time, kneeling on the floor, for him to do anything at all. I would stay in position even if he wasn't paying the slightest attention. Sometimes he would walk over and brush his fingers through my hair, rest them gently between my breasts, and my back would arch, and I would open more. Become more ready. Sometimes he would stroke the back of my head as he lay in the bed above me.

"Good girl, come up." he would say, a half-whisper, a soft purr. And I would stand from the floor and slip into the bed beside him. It took me so long to learn these moments were for him as much as they were for me.

# 5.

The last summer moon started glowing slick and wet in the sky just as he made me come. The sound of blood rushing in my ears, my come splashing into the floor, his fist between my legs. With careful hands and held breath, he moved back up my trembling body, kissing softly, pouring me back into the bed even though my legs were still dripping. He stroked me with a drenched hand, finding all the parts of me singing with pain and joy and the promise of marks and memories just blooming. He kissed them, flicked cold bite marks with his tongue. It made me moan as I shivered.

The bed drooling its duvet and pillows onto the floor, the moonlight cut up into sliver squares along the floor, reaching out to us, laid out. When he spoke, his voice was liquid, slow.

"It's like praying. Fucking you is like a revelation." He lay beside me, both of us slick with sweat and moonlight, breathless.

"Praying and fucking are both ways of talking without using your voice. Like writing a love letter."

He kissed my shoulder. Bit it softly like an apple.

"You have to have words to fuck, to pray, even if you don't speak them with your voice. You need words to offer."

The bedsheets were crisp, other descriptives for the feel of fabric are tooth and hand. I want his tooth and hand. But for a moment, I set aside arousal and just reverberated with the joy of being here, with him, beautiful and dirty and brutal and bright. Discordant, lush and lovely. The studio was dark, a faint red splash across the floor, the side of his face, from the darkroom light which I'd left on.

"What are the words you have?" he asked with a red-light smile.

"Yes, yes, yes…" I laughed, and it echoed.

"Are you mine?"

I was his, and I knew it.

"When I kneel on the floor," I said, rolling over in the sheets, "I knowingly kneel on the floor. It's not just with my body."

"You offer so much. Your hands and mouth, your cunt, and the bottoms of your feet, everything. But there is more. And I see it. You offer up your will, your permission." His hand was in my hair. He was looking up at the rafters. The red light caught on the fan of his eyelashes. "You offer up your will and your intelligence. Your imagination. You make a gift of all of it. And it's beautiful."

During the first crisp snap of autumn, he began to build the sculpture in earnest. Spending hours crafting the smaller pieces, tiny starbursts of mirror and glass, like fractal spores of the massive metal frame. Sorting and polishing shards of mirror and glass, beading endless little prisms onto spools and spools of fishing line, rainbows of colors dancing around on the walls as he worked in the sunset. He hung a rainstorm of mirror shards on near-invisible wires before the windows, glittering opposites to my drying natives at the other end.

Everything he did seemed purposeful, the same consuming focus as when he caned me, bit me. The work began to unfold before me. And one night, my skin still sore and humming, the tears still drying on my face, he kissed my shoulder tenderly and showed me the blueprints like being shown the inside of his mind.

He'd made currents over me with a Wartenberg wheel, jolts of light kicking all down my spine. My skin sang all over, and when I looked over his drawings, all the little points of light sang a little louder. This was intimacy more extraordinary than any nakedness, as great as my tears, my bruises. As though I had invited him to watch me take my portraits. He spread his sketches out over the bed, and I looked over all his erasures and smudges, coffee rings, notes legible only to himself.

"Light. And sharp edges everywhere. It will be almost too bright to look at, but all because of reflection, refraction. And Sharp. Deadly sharp. Between the light and knife-like edges of the glass…" He smiled. Wicked. Ran his hand down the curve of my naked hip.

"People are going to be afraid to go near it," I said with a smile. "But they will want to."

It looked like a city. Like a ship of wonders, something floating in a sky of cotton clouds, mysterious, dripping with prisms and imagination. A crystal cave, turned inside out, broken open like an egg. Unconstrained by reality, by what actually was or had or should have been.

As I looked over the drawings, he was touching me, his fingers curling around a nipple, his cock pressed between my legs, its length against me. Awake, hard. Gently, not wanting to pull either of us too far away from the pages, I turned, keeping him between my legs and kissed him softly, floating in a dark world of skin and clean, bright sheets and the pale pages tying to curl up.

He gripped my hips against him, not to wound or control me, but only to feel me in his hands, make sure I felt him. I parted my legs, and he pulled back and slid, hard and easy, inside me. It hurt a little from the power of him the night before, but my pleasure was greater. There was a little outer rim of pain and, deeper, a pleasure at the presence of his cock, filling, hardening more inside me. I pressed forward a little to meet it. He took me this way, slowly, until it was difficult for either of us to maintain the pace, want coiling up inside us.

"I want your mouth."

He slid out of me, and despite myself, I whimpered. But soon, I was kneeling between his knees, and I ran my hands gently, then hard, up his thighs. Drew my nails over his skin. I was hungry for him, desperate to touch him again. The head of his cock was jeweled with a drop of pre-come, slick from being inside me. I licked him clean, sucked his cock deep into my throat.

My hands were as active as my mouth. I listened to him gasp and growl, the pull of his fists in my hair. I kept him on edge with the variety of rhythms, the change from a handgrip of the entire cock to the lightest touch of the tip of it with my tongue. I know watching his cock slide into me was magnificent to him. Offering him pleasure made me flush with want, and the feeling of his cock rushing past my lips inflamed me.

I provoked him with my mouth, my eyes, my breasts. Shivering when my nipples brazed his thighs, desperate to touch myself, to curl my fingers inside myself, I could tell he liked to see me this way. I wanted to feel it, to know he was watching.

He gripped fistfuls of my hair and fucked my mouth, choking out my breath until there were tears in my eyes, rolling down my cheeks and dripping with my drool and spit onto his skin. He came hard, held me against him for a long time, tears on my cheeks falling onto his thighs. I smiled as his breath caught, steadied at the same rate as my own. As we both drifted in a haze. My mouth tasted like him. His hand reached out for mine.

Sometimes, reality overwhelmed me. A massive wave of absurdity and amazement. The simplest explanation is usually the right one, and my simplest explanation was he could read on my skin the hunger I had for him. Desire, which, by any other name, is the source of almost every sorrow, sorrow without visible expression. It was enough that he existed. That he looked at me and saw. He was proof of this: that my desires were not a prison but a temple. In such a state, I could accept nothing modest, no minor compromise. I wanted everything, all of him. I tried to swallow him with my mouth and my hands and my sex, grasping, fucking greedy. Hungry.

I can see that it was one thought among all the other ideas I had of him with a little distance. But it was a one I made an object. Turned over and over in my hand like a worry stone. A revelation: I didn't just want, I loved.

I wanted to, but I could not tell him. I did not trust this twist in the rope. I told Ruby at a booth in a diner off Yonge Street. Coffee, toast and scrambled eggs. As I talked, she worried at her necklace, ran the small triangle pendant back and forth over the chain. It wasn't really her opinion I wanted. I just wanted to say it out loud. Admit it to someone else. Speak the words in my own voice. The revelation was burning. But when I spoke this truth, she only smiled, a knowing look passing over her face.

"Of course you think that."

"You're making fun of me," I said.

"No—"

"Seriously?"

"I wasn't laughing," she said simply, putting down her coffee cup and measuring me with her gaze. "It's just, I knew when this started, that you would say it eventually."

"Fuck you."

"Honestly. I just knew."

"Way to be as reductive as possible."

"I mean, come on. You're both beautiful. You make art and fuck in a goddamn empty warehouse. Of course, you think you're in love with him. It's just that…"

"What?"

"Well, You're wrong. I mean, you know that, right? Even all caught up, you must suspect it."

"Suspect what?"

"Trust me, okay." She was smiling softly, but only halfway, and I hated her in that moment, a frank hot flush of hatred. "I know how it seems. And I don't mean this as some, you know, questioning of your judgment, or judgment of your experience, or whatever it is you do. I mean, your experience is totally valid."

"I'm feeling very validated."

"Listen, I'm not denying you feel something."

I made my eyes into slits and looked away from her. Outside traffic was passing, the clouds moved, quick and grey.

"But you have known for ages how you feel about him—he inspires you as an artist, you make him coffee, and he makes you come. All of this is wonderful. And, yes, it's rare. And up till now, you hadn't made that link to being in love with him because, well, everything was so new. But now it's not, so there is this…"

"This is not an attempt to recapture the novelty."

"That's not what I was going to say, smartass."

She took a sip of coffee, a small smile playing over her lips. Whatever anger I was simmering in, I was feeling it alone.

"I was only saying that love won't make it real. I mean, he makes your blood boil, but loving him won't make it hotter. Or more real."

"That's not what's happening."

"Has he ever even taken you to a movie?"

"God," I said. "No. But it's not like I have wanted to go on a date."

"Exactly. Loving him will avail you nothing. Not in a real way." She laughed a little. "I mean, what are you going to do, marry him?"

"No..." I laughed too, but it was short, hard and angry. I was glad to be angry because if I wasn't, I was worried I might cry.

"Right? This is just adding another level of risk. And that isn't love."

I nodded.

"I'm really wondering whether there can actually be love there," Ruby said, her tone shifting into something abstract, necklace sliding. "So far from its natural habitat. It seems like that's part of a different story for you. Another time. A consequence for different choices."

"Why deny this?" I asked. Angry and showing it.

"The only person I care about here is you." Her voice was serious again, and she dropped her pendant to reach out for my hand.

"I know you. I love you. I don't give a shit about this guy. And"—she showed her bottom lip, looked away, looked back at me like she was making herself—"he hits you, babe. No matter what you say, no matter how good it is for you right now, that means something. I get it. It's hot, its wild. But still. He's not your boyfriend, right? I don't want to see you throw yourself needlessly in harm's way with your heart, too. I do not deny your feelings, I'm just asking questions."

"You know that is a really shitty thing to say." I pulled my hand away, held on to my coffee cup for dear life. Her expression was tight, concerned, and I tried to soften my tone. "If someone told you in a really reasonable way, that you weren't feeling what you were feeling, would you believe them?"

"I don't know."

I didn't finish my breakfast.

There were moments in bed with him when affection and delight crackled out of us like thunder at the tattered end of a storm. His arm curled around me. Our bodies beyond the need to seek expression or sensation or satisfaction, simply at peace. Actively in the moment. Slick with sweat and the scent of each other, he rested his hand gently on the small of my back. There wasn't more. That moment was full of everything. Echoes of pain and pleasure, of every touch, the promise of the future, like an avalanche, waiting. At that moment, I was completely myself, my lips salty with tears shed in joy and pain.

I said nothing about it to Ruby.


It wouldn't be unreasonable to wonder how knowing I loved him changed all the torrid violence and lust we shared, primarily as this truth remained unspoken between us. It would be acceptable to think things remained essentially the same. But I felt as if I was finally awake.

I remembered his words all those months earlier before he kissed me and smiled. A warning. In this new waking world, everything was sharp and clear, vivid. The shape of my desires made sense. They were answered by his. I had hope, suddenly, in a general way. Love opened a door in my body, my heart, into a deeper place where all sensation was immensely titillating, where memories shimmered with a depth of emotion I never suspected I possessed. Whimpering in pain as he fucked me, his hands hard on my throat, my hips, tangled in my hair, everything was part of this secret world that lived between us, where every gasping breath was full of joy.

Ruby was right; I did not imagine a winter wedding, a family in a farmhouse, I did not build an elaborate and complex story out of our lives, no future around the idea of him. Instead, I inhabited every moment we had, I embodied them. I imprinted myself with sensation and memory. All the moments that he existed in my presence, and I in his, were laced with ease even when they were brutal. Everything took on the hue of the beautiful. I would have to remind myself fog did not roll in, the moon did not rise, just for us.

I could not have dreamed of such happiness. For years, my desire was exiled to a barren territory of denial. I knew as the truth lay unspoken against my chest when it was potential rather than actual. I wondered if any of it could be real. I built my photos, imagining entire worlds and their histories, and out of love and pain and pleasure, I made hope for myself.

If you'd told this story of falling in love, I would have assured you this person was reckless, dangerous. That it was fiction. But it wasn't. This was my life, and I was happy and in love, and every moment seemed like an inevitable manifestation of beauty. Bright with brutality and prolonged involuntary waves of ecstasy. For so long, I thought this kind of sensation was an impossible color, a preposterous dream.

But fate is a trickster, I remembered. Did I dare say anything to him? There was too much risk, my life very literally in his hands, my heart in his fists. Ruby was right about that much. I struggled, viciously, to understand the sensation of love, slow awakening of the seriousness of my condition.

We didn't share some conventional unconsummated love affair, no flirtatious exchange with a stranger in a train station, no tender cautious trespass, fraught with boundary and limitation, no summer blockbuster romance. This was torrid made flesh. So, I didn't say a word. But I tried to speak the truth with my touch, to open me from breast to belly, to offer him all the wildness of my body.

Standing at his drafting table, I marveled again at the precision of his drawings. My eyes sought out new notes written in that same sharp pencil.

"What do you think?" he asked me, putting his hand on mine.

"Of course," I said, and he looked at me, brow furrowed. "I look at it, and it feels inevitable."

He looked up at me with copper almond eyes, wide.

"Does it look like—what? Do you like it?"

How to answer, when mostly I was feeling his hand

touching mine. It looked like how it felt to be touched by him.

"It is beautiful. But It's just the map," I said. "Seeing it in real life will be different. Like you said. Bright and sharp."

"A map." He smiled and nodded. "These are the pieces, the atoms and cells…" He gestured at the stacks of broken glass and mirror, the strands and patterns of crystals hanging in rows from fishing line. "But now there are other, bigger things to build. The thing itself," He grinned. "My agent wants a video of the progress."

"Could you film it? I thought we could put a camera inside, film the assembly that way. It's going to take weeks"

"It's a wonderful idea," I said. "Something inside, looking out. We could put a little motion sensor on it, leave it synced to a computer here, so we don't have to set it up every time you work on it." I traced the lines with my finger. He crinkled his eyes in his most endearing smile and kissed me hard. I felt so many things at once. Flushed and blooming with excitement, but also fear. Again and again, boundaries were broken. I would let him break them because I wanted him to break them.

"You see why? I don't tell you what is monstrous or beautiful, just like I don't tell you what to love, how to fuck, how to kiss. But I understand what you imagine because it is what I imagine too."

He was standing up straight, arms crossed over this chest, looking down at the drawings, over my shoulder.

"Because each of us has dreams and nightmares…"

"Yes."

"And this." He moved his hand in the air, covering the sculptures frame, the scattering of small workstations around it. "It needs to be a collision of harmonious perspectives. Light from everywhere, to everywhere. I want everyone to see themselves in it. Like the mirrors, reflecting us back at ourselves. Desire and pain.... Mirrors and truth." He smiled his predator smile.

Autumn settled with a sway of cold rain and fresh grey skies. Every weekend, every spare evening, or afternoon, when I could pull myself away from work, I would spend hours in the studio, sometimes only watching silently, kneeling or making him coffee, peeling his oranges.

We took turns bringing dinner. Breadsticks and cream crackers, tiny pickles, exotic cheese, salted oatmeal cookies, extravagant bars of Italian chocolate. In those early fall days, there was a new side of him: obsessive and even more intense. I fell quickly in love with this single-minded man, not only because I was included inside his contagious creativity.

"I think we need more shards here, more, layered, like steps, no? I'm trying to decide whether the shards should be actually dangerously sharp—what do you think. Make them draw a little blood."

I smiled, and he did too. "It should hurt to touch."

I watched him and his mirror ball explosion and saw myself that everything was possible. He spent his time sewing together silver and glass strands, gluing mirror beads like drops of dew, sculpting orbs and flowers out of broken crystal, and stringing them onto twisted wires. Some days, I would come in and he would be listening to recordings of cricket sounds, distant warble of night songbirds, animal-in-the-undergrowth noises, night's lonely songs.

I reserved my photos, my work, for myself. Which isn't to say that I hid them from him. Only that, unlike his firework of glass and light, I worked mostly in the dark, often when he wasn't there. I waited, held back, and after he was gone, I would play my music loud. Once I took Polaroids of myself in the dark room's red light and then on his drafting table. The images blurry and dark, partial—a glint of my face and moving hair, the curve of my hip, the black triangle of my public hair.

With my camera, I made photos in the early morning, flat grey light. Pictures of my hands reaching around me from all angles, images of myself scattered over the floor. I developed and carved them in the evenings. Creating manual composite pictures of my legs and arms forgotten in my empty bedroom, my left hand abandoned on a bookshelf.

I was a woman in pieces, moving toward a whole. My form with hands reaching between my thighs, holding the swell of my waist, gripping one breast, covering my eyes.

I was in my life, in life. I was alive. Awake. Sleeping Beauty, awake from a long sleep, ready to bleed again. Scattered through the castle, always ready to bleed for him. I was his. His.

And suddenly aware, almost in a panic—of the wealth

of possibility in the world. Within myself. In my everyday life, my phone calls to my mother, the occasional dinner with friends, morning walks to the coffee shop, everything was changed even though no one noticed it.

I felt all this with a fresh searing honesty. I felt and felt and felt. In those heady days when winter threatened to snap shut around autumn, I felt everything. One evening we walked hand in hand to a late-night bakery for hot chocolate, then began the long walk all the way back to my front door. The dark sky streaked with long narrow clouds, tattered on their edges. There was a smell of earth, soil, rich and dark leaves rotting as we passed the cemetery on Winchester Street where'd he first kissed me in the car. I felt like a ravenous wolf; I wanted to devour the world, to be greedy, to be sated. He laughed when my fingers squeezed his, and he squeezed back.

"What do you want for your art?" he asked. "Your photos are evolving so beautifully. Do you want to show them, or do you only make them for yourself?"

"I don't really think about it."

"They are so challenging," he said. The last clinging leaves rustled in the breeze over us, and sometimes drops of water fell on our shoulders.

"You see them, I suppose," I said. "You watch as they go from big stacks of photos down to one image. You walk up and spend time with them. I don't know. I think you see something other people don't. It's enough, though, I think." I shrugged, sipped my hot chocolate. "No one would see them like you do."

"Why won't you show them to anyone?"

"I do want them for myself. But I want other things too." I admitted. "That isn't why I don't show them. I'm just afraid I think."

"You seem wonderfully calm in your life. As though it's all in order. As though there is nothing that you require. But you are ravenous. Sometimes, I touch you, and I can feel it. Jaws that snap."

"I am. I'm starving."

"I know." He nodded. "You know, you can ask for what you need."

"Need?" I laughed, but I was serious, and he could see it. "That's a complicated word. Who needs anything, really, besides food and water? Shelter to watch the storm. I have much more than I need."

"Then how can you be ravenous?" He looked at me for a long time, expression easy, empty of judgment as ever. Kissed my forehead.

"It's more to say, maybe I am unsatisfied."

"I can't think of you that way. It seems contrary to how I know you. It doesn't make sense to me. You have all this talent, everything is waiting for you. What are you waiting for?"

"Life," I admitted with a whisper. "Death. All of it. Everything. Maybe I'm not waiting. Maybe I've always felt like I needed permission."

"You don't." He said, his voice surprised, almost dismissive. He kissed me then, and his mouth tasted like chocolate.

# 6.

The next day was too warm for fall, a day hot and still as ash. When I arrived at the studio and slid the door open on its massive wheels, it was too silent. Nothing. I hung up my jacket and bag and I walked from one end of the studio to the other, moving slowly. I felt like a stranger, one who would have flushed to know the things said and done in the neatly made bed. Even neatly made, it looked glaring, sinful. Out of place and therefore screaming in its obscenity.

"Beautiful." I whispered in the empty room.

I remembered it exactly, great dust-dancing beams of evening light, the studio smelled of glue and glass dust, developer and stopper fluid. I made coffee and drank it sprawled across the white linen horizon and wondered, with crystal clarity, how all of this would end.

How long was happiness anyway?

He called my name as he walked in, stepped swiftly across the room, light-footed. His expression was open and bright, a smile, a kind of new focus.

"I have news."

"Positive?"

"Everything. Today everything is positive." He kissed me on the forehead, took my hand. "Make us some coffee, and I will tell you."

I set out our mugs and spoon, boiled water to pour over the grounds. He reclined in his chair.

"I was in New York for maybe 36 hours."

I smiled at the idea of him standing on a steamy street corner. Gloved hands in his jacket pockets. Art, I knew. It was the only reason he would go like that, sudden, without a word. Like I did during an active season.

"Did you get lucky?"

He smiled with a wicked grin.

"With the sale? Not yet. But it looks good. I mean, this week, one promise, the next week, a different one. But it's promising. There is a trend. But that isn't the news."

The water boiled, the familiar glug in the matte black kettle, I poured out. The smell of coffee slowly filled the studio.

"Before I left, I'm having a meal with a friend of mine who is an artist, an outstanding artist; she makes sculptures—sexy, very obscene, everything in bronze. She made this urn you would love. Very elaborate, like six feet tall, baroque. Covered in these glazes from old porn magazines. Filthy, beautiful. Anyway, she wanted me to meet this other woman, a curator, opening an exhibition of some new gallery in Brooklyn. Old combine manufacturing plant or something. Massive space, apparently. Industrial, just like here."

"And she wanted to meet you?"

He laughed. "No. She had no idea who I was. But she knows my friend, bless her, and my friend is very clever. In this offhand way, she tells her I'm looking for a gallery, a big space to show my newest piece. Tells her all about the Piano, how this was bigger even. She said it casual like I was shopping around all these galleries in town. Like that's why I was there."

"It is good enough for its own gallery and more. It should be in a museum." I said, laughing, his smile was contagious.

"Look who's talking."

"Anyway." I said and handed him a cup of coffee and he brushed his hand over mine, kissed it, gestured for me to sit. "It would be amazing, an entire gallery for you. It's huge step."

"Can you imagine?" He asked me, sipping his coffee.

"Yes." I could. "Easy."

How wonderfully right for him. I thought of his fingers as he wove chains out of silver. The piece was going to be everything he thought it was and more. It was going to be a symphony. I could see it, hanging in an empty room, lit mostly by light trapped in its reflections, and I knew the only correct thing for him would be to take it where it could be seen. Even if that was far away from me.

"It hasn't happened." He said, carefully. "It may not happen. But I think she liked me. She took my name, gave me her information. She found me online. She wants to meet again. You'll need to shoot the work soon, I think."

I nodded. I knew, of course, how could I not. And I knew as well this would take him from me, that I would be left behind. And if not now, then soon. I could not feel any of the human things suggested by the thought. Not grief or sadness. Not yet. I wanted the world to see what he created the same way I wanted his teeth on my throat, his hand in mine. I could deny him nothing. To try was to act against myself, my will as well as my desire. I would be sad later, when this was done.

"We're waiting, for now. She's suggested a meeting in a few days, it's almost confirmed. They want to put together a press kit for the piece. If she makes an offer, our situation could change quickly."

"Everything," we said at the same time, and we both smiled. After all the moments that lived between us, naked energetic want, tears, sweat and come, you would think it would be easy to say: *I love you…*

"So much to do before we get there." He put down his mug on a stack of art books in a milk crate and moved forward, knelt on the knotted rug before my chair.

"I might have to leave you." When he spoke again, his voice was kind and soft in a way I seldom heard it. Sincere. I wondered if it was sad. "But please remember, no matter what happens, or where I end up going with this. Please, my girl, if I send for you, please come."

I tried to find the words to say *yes*. To say *I love you*, nice and simple. But I could only nod my head. He kissed my forehead and tucked a strand of hair behind my ear.

"And there is still so much time before I'll need to go."

But there wasn't.


A week later, I arrived at the studio with my camera and gig bag to photograph his sculpture. I was there to photograph the piece in progress, as I had in the time before I knew him.

Only now, it would be so vastly different.

Partly hoping, as I walked up the stairs, that the studio would be as we left it. But I knew it wouldn't be. In the stairwell there were sounds of a small crowd. Evenly paced

ambient music, chatter, banging. There was the movement
of life, not our life, but something else. Our territory was so
insular it felt like a violation that this first brush of our
separation should come with a crowd. His agent, an
interviewing journalist, a gallery rep and all of them would
have interns, assistants. Only the artists typically work
alone.

As I walked down the corridor, I thought again about
what I would do with the lighting, how to manage
reflections of the set up given the endless refraction of the
surfaces, if I even wanted to try to hide the camera. I
thought perhaps the photos might be more intreating, more
honest, if one saw the camera. Would it be possible to view
the piece in a gallery without seeing oneself? I was planning
to shoot mostly from the floor to suggest its size and scope
and I wanted shots with the ladders and support struts in
place, the way I saw it all the time, to show the progress and
its delicacy, it's becoming. I'd asked him in advance to lay
out his tools.

No one heard me roll open the door except for him. He
saw me right away and looked up, everyone around him was
busy and for a moment it was just the two of us, looking at
each other across the distance. I stood with the door sliding
closed behind me and we faced each other and smiled,
connected. I bowed my head softly.

Next, to him, a woman was talking, huge red glasses
reflecting the screen she was reading from, curly ringlets of
grey hair bouncing with her laugh. When she noticed that
he wasn't responding, she looked up at him, then at me,
nodded.

"The camera's here." She called down the studio to the little cluster of people gathered around the armchairs, though no one was sitting down. She turned around, walked into the small crowd. He looked at me and we both smiled the same smile.

I set up quickly with minimal lighting, primarily softening the reflections so I wouldn't have to cut the brightness, controlling what ambient light was there. He was caught up at the center of a clutch of people, in the dim light, huddled around the camera as though it would tell them something. They moved off when I started shooting, watching carefully. I was used to this, the kind of spectator sport that a photoshoot could become.

The woman with the red glasses talked almost constantly but whenever I looked up, he was watching me. He was dressed in a black dress shirt with the sleeves rolled up, arms tattooed and shadowed in the gloom I was creating to limit the reflections. He looked menacing, beautiful. I could tell some of the agent's people were giving him a lot of space. At one point, changing a battery and scrolling through the memory card the agent came up to me, offered me a glass of wine in a little opaque plastic flute. I shook my head, raised the camera by way of explanation. She stood beside me, and we watched a few others carefully moving around the sculpture with glass cleaner and soft white clothes, white cotton gloves covering hands and wrists. I realized everyone near it was whispering and it made me smile. I took several shots of this before the agent spoke.

"He's such a rake, this one. A bed right in the studio. And those photos! where do you think he got them?" She arched an eyebrow at me, nodding toward my portraits along the back wall. "Imagine being a woman and coming in here and seeing all this. Would you still fuck him?"

"Yes," I said, deadpan, and she laughed a bright crackle of sound, drew on a rose quartz vaporizer, exhaled a plume of sweet-smelling mist. I moved away without another word and shot over a little less than an hour. When I packed up to leave everyone else was still talking, planning. Someone had opened a bottle of wine.

Suddenly his hand was on my wrist, turning me around, lifting the camera bag from my shoulder and setting it on the floor at our feet. The room vanished as he stood before me, back to the little group of people, hiding me from their view. From within the folds of his jacket, he produced one of the white polishing cloths they were using on the sculpture. Carefully, he wiped away my red lipstick.

"I am doing this because I want to, not because I do not like the color." He whispered to me, lifting my face up to his, "I want to touch your mouth."

He smiled, his eyes on my lips.

"It is a lovely color. It looked beautiful on you."

His voice was steady and warm but close. It touched me like his hands, and I felt radiant.

"Thank you." I bowed my head, smiled.

"Come back in two hours?"

It was said quietly, but his voice always made my knees weak. The way he could say *kneel*, no matter how he phrased it.

"Of course." My gaze found his. And for the only time that afternoon, I was happy I was there, present. He was looking into me rather than at me, into the place glowing under his gaze. My heart raced as his hand found mine, held it. Squeezed.

"It will be better when they are gone."

He lifted my hand to his mouth and kissed my palm, his teeth catching lightly on the meat of my thumb, and I almost whimpered. There was such naked desperation in his voice, a coiled edge that marked us as allies. Keepers of a secret. Someone called him back to the group.

Leaving, I peered one last time through toward the distant pools of light where he was standing in a swirl of voices and activity. Layouts of the gallery somewhere far away unspooled over his drafting table. He was lost to me. I could see nothing but a shimmering blur, the searing afterimage of the sculpture when I closed my eyes.


Two hours later, I knelt naked on the hard knotted rug, my body trained up on his words like hooks. My wrists were tied to my ankles, my body bowed out, back arched, exposing my breasts, undersides thrust up, pearly white in the dim light. He smacked them, hard. My skin flushed pink, then red. Dark torture that made me gasp.

Want. From time to time, he shifted my thighs farther apart and smacked me again. Slow, slow. Impact measured and steady. His voice fell on me like his hands. He told me to breathe. Using his voice, he guided me through pain as surely as his hands created it, his voice like a bright light through the frantic darkness that threatened to overwhelm me.

"Stay." He said, soft and tender as his hands were murderous. "Stay with me. Breathe."

I did, I focused my breath, my gaze, I found him in the hectic buzzing storm of pain...

"Good girl."

The slapping stopped, and his hands became feathers, drifting over the static of pain over my skin. He calmed me with tender touches. He flicked my nipple with humming hot fingers, and finally, finally, he pulled off his clothes, and as he did, he stopped to make me kiss the side of his cock, pressed it hard and hot against my cheek, finding a glide against my cheek, my mouth. Hot and thick, a steady, sure comfort and a threat.

# 7.

He was going to leave. I knew this, of course. But first, there was the filming. My last role in his piece. His impending absence shone, and I held our work and sex and the snarl of our kisses as gels to tint the light a more desirable color. I was going to remember us, and we were going to shine. I wanted to tell him, but instead we talked about the sculpture.

"It's going to look like something from another world."

"Do you think it will work?" he asked, and I nodded. He smiled and closed his hand around my throat, firm. A solid grip closing. I looked in his eyes, a long gaze as he pulled my body toward him. He turned me around, moving me where he wanted, how he wanted, and bit the back of my neck. Brutal, his jaws trembling not to bite me too hard. I felt the pain, but also a deep calming shiver rolled down my spine. He pressed his body into mine, his teeth sinking into me until I gasped. Whimpered.

"You're so bright, shining..." he said, digging his fingers into the spaces between my ribs, holding me against him. "I wish you could see it."

"It's you," I said, gasped really, forming words around pain. "You see what you make of me. A reflection of your own light."

Like love, pain creates moments in which identity can be altered and changed. Because of this, masochism isn't only about the senses; it is also about identity. Masochism isn't only a subjective personal sensory experience; it is also a communal one. A story told between bodies.

"We become new creatures, you and I." He said, speaking into my skin. "Over and over. Building and ruining and building again many selves, each of them explored, loved, felt. It's not me or you. Two mirrors, reflecting each other's light."

Through him, I found emotional experiences I didn't believe myself capable of. I became aware of new rooms and chambers inside the mansion of my heart. I saw an entirely new spectrum of emotion, a surprising new vividness to all my senses. The pain he gave me was like a layer of revelation, a bright, sharp complexity.

"How could I feel this, experience us, and not be changed?"

He kissed me, pinned me to him. Nothing essential was missing. There was nothing to struggle to understand, only experience.

After we fucked, we made tea and watched the sunset. He filmed the sinking rad flare with his phone, sending the video to the folder on drive where the sculptured construction was being slowly documented. After a little while as I got dressed to leave, he pulled me down to him again and kissed me hard.

"If I said to come with me, if I wanted you to meet this agent again, would you?"

I laughed, but we both knew it was only a way for me to look away.

"I think your work is…"

I shook my head, kissed him, stopping his words. "That's not right. This is your time," I said and smiled. He was silent, looking me over.

"Do you remember what is said? if I send for you…"

"Yes, of course. If you send for me, I will come. But you need to go be famous." I smiled, curled my hands against his chest and tried to imagine meeting him in some other city, some other time. I wondered if he actually would, or if this was just easier than saying goodbye.

"I'm going to miss you." He kissed me again, with something I had not felt from him before. Something soft. A kind of naked urgency without crushing dominance, just steady taking of satisfaction, desire. In this kiss, I was not who I thought I was to him; I did not know myself at all.

But it didn't matter, really. When his hands moved to rest on my skin, warm, hot, like stones in the sun, it was enough. It was enough just to be naked with him, beside him. As though I could be everything.


A few days later, he was back in New York, and I was alone in the studio. The last marks he'd given me were healing and I'd been avoiding the space. My knees weren't bruised any more. I knew he was busy, getting the final piece ready to move and I couldn't bear to be there and know he was leaving. I delayed locking up for the night and going home, instead I kept the lights low. I watched evening roll over the studio and saw grief rolling on the horizon, bloom in my chest, wafting inside me so it was hard to breathe.

Full of a slow agitation I stripped off my clothes. I had been naked so many times in this space, sobbing and trembling and laughing, wet with desire, animal and human sounds of love and pleasure and pain dripping out of me with come and sweat. But never alone. Alone, I moved around silently, my newest photos still dripping dry in the darkroom.

A dizzy spiral of my reflections appeared on the mirror skin of his sculpture, almost complete now, tossing around the light in the dim space, catch every scrap and drop of brightness and casting it around its skin. Aggressively screaming its beauty to the empty room. Its sharp, dangerous perfection. The chains twinkled and glittered, sighing under the weight they bore. Hard, vivid light, bright and angry when I gazed at it. I moved around it, drunk on its light and dangerous edges and all the ways I would miss it, and as the sun set it seemed to strain and reach for me.

*Please, please…*

*Let me touch you…*

Watching my reflection shatter and spray around the sculpture, my body was robbed of its logic and order. Lacking familiar construction, I saw myself as never before. A rail of the collar bone, the swell of fat on my hip, the notch and cliffs of my ribs, the slight hollow above my belly button, the narrowing of a wrist. Everything decontextualized. It was a beautiful sculpture, and it screamed its beauty out from all its bright sharp edges. Its beauty was in the motion, and in all the pieces of a thing seen at just the right angles, just the right speed. The many vesseled view offered a kind of visual truth, perhaps this was the true property of space, a method to reconcile countless points of view.

I wondered, turning so pieces of me cascaded in turning, if this was what he saw. When he crushed and slapped and broke me open under his hands, when he coaxed my surrender or an orgasm or tears, played like an instrument, was this what he saw, a river of moving moments.

Shining. A thousand beautiful contradictions. It looked like a bleeding heart of light, a ship floating in all that was possible but not yet become. In a dizzied state, as though hypnotized, I moved forward, nearer and nearer to the glowing, floating structure.

I lay down on the sweet clean floor under the sculpture, feeling the knots of the scarred hardwood under my shoulder blades, rocking my pelvis forward as solid above me was the light, sharp, glass spears and knives. The sculpture was a sun made swords and mirrors, casting shadows and reflections on the walls and my skin in the half-light.

I didn't close my eyes. I kept them open, watching knife edges of light dripping down on me. Carefully, slowly, almost so I did not know I was doing it, I reached up with my right hand and softly, and brushed curled fingers over my nipple. A gentle tug of sadness and pleasure trembled in me, a delicious, slightly sickening kind of loneliness, like loss, a wafting smoke of grief and comfort.

My touch grew more sure, more steady, my hands explored my body. For a time, it was almost an intellectual exploration, watching reflections ripple up around me as though I was sinking in water. My fingertips gently traced my ribs, jaw and throat, my mouth, my collarbones, my breasts and stomach, around the constriction of my pelvis and the softness of my thighs, over and over. My fingers found the curled flush textures of my sex, feeling out its steady and subtle transformations, filling, flush with bloom.

My sex was dripping wet, my fingers stirring, damp. Memories of us wafted off my skin, rippled over me the way my reflection caressed the sculpture's mirrored skin. I became my own shining world of sensation, withering in pleasure, draining its blood with teasing fingers. My hand between my legs, I stroked my clit, slid two fingers inside and began to rub my clit against my curled palm. Moving forward, I felt my hand curl in my cunt, and when I fell back, the pressure shifted forward. A sensation of fullness gathered. The approach moved me. Shook me like a doll, everything surfacing into a hard orgasm.

I came as I watched myself in the mirrors, a thousand pieces, none of them whole, all sharp edges and angles, my body glistening with light and sweat, my hands moved, the honey of my lust shining on my hands, my thighs, shining, wetness dripping between my legs. And every part of me, every scrap and shard, glowed with pleasure.

That night I sobbed in the shower, locked away from the world by tile and glass, scalding water rolling over the fading bruises on my thighs. I gave up to the future all my moments of love and grief. I cried to slow the corrosion of his memory of me, the increasing comfort of past tense.

I remembered his words that afternoon so many months ago:

*It is different for you. This is extra in your real life, a dream on the fringes…but for me, this is it. This is everything.*

But he didn't mean me. I sobbed with big desperate gulps of air, pathetic curling whimpers, and wondered how it was our positions had become so horribly reversed. I cried myself out, head split from pain, my eyes sore. How beautiful, I thought as the water turned cold, to feel oneself open, transparent, to see oneself reflected so perfectly in another. But to allow yourself to be seen by one person, to be reflected, was to risk distortion, ruin, when they looked away.

And then—

He was gone.

He left on a Wednesday, the man I loved.

The sky was gloaming when I arrived to the studio after I knew he would be gone. I hadn't been there for a week; I didn't want to see him pack up the space, to see the men with crates and nail guns boxing up the sculpture.

Muted light reflected off a mass of impenetrable clouds gathering slowly in the sky overhead as I walked the length of the space, even more empty, echoing. I still felt him there, and my sadness was the same color as the strange early twilight light. His end of the studio was empty. As though he'd never been there at all. The floor swept and polished, all his coffee cups gone. The chairs, the table, the bed all remained like the witness to a crime. With the sculpture gone, the space seemed even more massive. Almost new. The ladders and his table and rug had vanished. Suddenly the studio accumulating a tangle of emotions. It wasn't easy to be there.

My photos were gone.

The strands of fishing wire where I hung them trembled like spider's silk in their nakedness. Gone. As though they were never there. And suddenly, looking at all the space where they were supposed to be, where he was supposed to be, grief for all I lost rushed in and consumed me.

Later, my face swollen and tight from crying, I lay on the floor where his black knotted rug would have been. It was cold on the floor, and my skin was tight with goosebumps even though I was fully dressed. I stayed there until I began to shiver, glad to feel the cold and not the sudden massive maw of confusion that opened up all around me. He lingered in the place like a ghost. The contradiction. The violation. And still, my body shook with a loss of its own. Still, I missed him almost more than I could stand.

Unlike the pain of a slap or the bite of rope or the stroke of a cane, this pain offered no arousal, no complicated enjoyment, no illumination. This pain's lesson was brutal, and mostly I wanted to avoid learning it. Consensual pain has a dark and beautiful gravity, a patient observant will. It allowed me to play with power that was mine and not mine, mine again.

A paradox.

I learned a lot from pain. I learned to see my life, theoretically, as a crossing place for several systems and ideas and memories, all connected. It allowed me to see myself as a construct of desire. Is that power or obsession?

You cannot talk about one without talking about the other.

But this wasn't consensual pain.

I watched the first snow of the year begin to fall, knots of lace against the glass. Cold kissed against my fingers, and I curled them into fists at my sides. I sat there for a long time in silence. There was nowhere to go with this kind of sadness, and just like that, I knew all over what I lost—a home I did not realize I had until it was gone. And my images, complete and polished.

He told me we would only have a little while. He said that he would leave. I knew it, even if I tried not to think about it, even if I never applied the fact to how I felt, how I would feel.

He told me he would hurt me.

Slowly, I watched the snow turn to rain. The drops got bigger, icy cold creeping along the floor, a cold cousin to grief, who hung close, too close, and I knew I should go home, that I should put on my clothes and stay warm…

*Take care of yourself.*

I heard it in his voice, settling on my chest, rough against my skin. It almost made me cry all over again, but I still knew it was right. I ached with it. With love, that was withering with loss.

I was glad we never talked about it. A chill ran through my body. I wondered how long it would be before I felt the fullness of what he did to me, what I let him do to me. I rested my hand against my cheek in a vague approximation of his touch and wondered how long it would take me to hate him.

Walking to the subway, still cold right down into my bones, I tried to understand how I could have been so deceived, so far gone? The train tracks glowing bright against the dark of gravel and concrete. He left on a Wednesday. I would be stunned for days by the simplicity of it, amazed the world continued. Just a day of the week. The effortless beauty between us was gone.

Like my photos.

Vanished.

I tried to find the logic, the reason or the method behind it but could not.

*I will never see him again.* I whispered out the window to the snow

But I didn't believe it.

Not really.


I hadn't seen Ruby since she rejected my confession, but she called a few days after he left and, wearing my bathrobe and with unwashed hair, I'd rashly promised to visit on Saturday without considering if I was going to be able to keep the sorrow from spilling out of me. On Friday night, I stayed at the studio until almost midnight—not working on anything, not touching anything. I didn't look at where my stacks of finished photos should have been. I didn't touch my tools, my knives. I didn't bother to check to make sure my equipment and negatives were still there. He took nothing else. All I lost was love and my art. My art. I wondered if I ever called it that before,

I lay in the bed, his bed, fully clothed, my coat and bag boots in a messy heap by the door, the duvet puffed up around me. I moved the words around in my mouth.

*My art.*

*My art…*

*Mine.*


On Saturday morning, after a run along the river that failed to clear my head, I walked over to Ruby's carrying some peonies from the flower shop on the corner and some cookies I made instead of crying on my kitchen floor. I told her he left, but I didn't tell her about my photos. I couldn't bring myself to admit to such a complex reality of shame and hurt. I watched her reflection in her kitchen window as she put the flowers in water and made us cloudy English tea. Ruby spent too long arranging the cookies on a plate.

"Did you tell him you loved him, after?" She asked, sitting down at the table with me, and a long silence lapsed between us. Her tone suggested a kind of defeat, as though she had hoped not to acknowledge the subject hung between us with the heavy smell of the flowers.

"No." My voice was icy, and I couldn't help it. "I suppose you could say I took your advice."

"I'm sorry," she said with a sigh. Her hands drifted apart and then folded in her lap. "I forgot how it can be when you're in love. What I said…it was…"

She reached across the table and rested her hand over mine, her fingers closing around my hand, and I closed my eyes, using the darkness to build a damn around the sadness that pushed against them. He did that to me once, reached across a table and held my wrist so hard it hurt.

"I forgot. And when I thought about it after, I thought, maybe I forgot on purpose."

"What do you mean?" I opened my eyes to look at her.

"When you talked about him, you were so happy. You were so out, so open. It was like—I don't know, I don't even think you saw it. How different you were. And it made me… jealous? Is that weird? I mean not for what you're doing but that you felt something so powerful."

I pulled my hand away. Hers retreated and curled back around her cup as though to keep them warm. Mine became fists. I looked out her window again: no reflections, just endless sky.

"When you told me, about the…well, about you." She looked at me from under her lashes, glanced away. "I was scared for you. Maybe I'm puritanical." She laughed, and I smiled, did my best. "But it was so good for you, and I just…" she sighed, "…I just didn't understand, and I didn't behave well. I'm sorry."

Her shoulders collapsed around her, and she hugged her arms, smiled, arranged the cookies again, pushed the plate toward me. I knew it was hard to admit. It was probably easier for her to call me insane, unhinged, than to wonder if she was wrong. I nodded, unsure at first if I could do anything else. I did not trust myself to speak or move, or look at her. It was too much. The grief of loss, her need for forgiveness, my own reluctance to tell her anything. I picked up a cookie, cracked it in half and handed one half to her. I ate the other silently.

"We were not right," I said, trying hard not to cry, a sob lodged in my throat like a sharp stone. After a moment, I started to laugh, but it sounded too much like a broken sob, and I stopped. Ruby cleared her throat and recrossed her ever-moving hands, looked at the flowers and sighed.

"Let's go for a walk." I offered and broke another cookie in half.

We walked through the blustering wind along the uneven breakwater along the lake. Swooping gulls laughed as they dove after each other into the black surf. At one point, we stopped and watched the waves, and Ruby looped her arm in mine. Standing with her, it seemed so obvious; if you wanted transparency, you needed the courage to be honest. There was no guarantee others would be honest with you, but what choice did you have? He told me he was going to hurt me, but I had to fall in love anyway.

"Will you see him again?"

"No, it's impossible to speak to him now. There is too much between us."

Not impossible. I knew where he was. I could find the gallery without trouble. I remembered my resolve that I would never see him again.

I must, I determined, to reach as best I could for what was real, what I really thought and wanted, separate from all the tangled unknown from what he had done. I wondered if it was possible to cut off loving him from the

woman I was when I loved him, from all the things I wanted
and received. If I would lose her too…

"Are you doing alright?" Ruby asked, and I almost
smiled. Almost laughed.

"In what sense?"

"You look…tired, sad. Like you haven't been sleeping."

But I had been sleeping. I had been sleeping for hours
and hours, at strange times, as though to escape the truth
that hunted me, the questions that haunted me throughout
the day. *Why?*

"I'm alright." I nodded.

What words are there for this? What metaphor could
there be? I lost everything in one motion, and like every slap
and punch and cane stroke, I only sighed and bowed my
head and let fate fall. There were no words, no way to make
her see, to help her understand it. So, I said nothing about
it at all. I lied instead.

"It feels like something separate from my life now." It
was all I could say.

"That's a good way to put it. Separate from life. That's
good. It's better that way. It was just something that
happened. You'll look back when you're an old woman and
be amazed you were so wild. So brave."

She squeezed my arm and laughed, watching the birds
fly against the wind. She misunderstood.

"Protecting your heart is the most important thing."

"My heart?" I felt and sounded genuinely surprised.

*I am hurt.* I wanted to scream. *My heart is ruined.*

"I don't mean… It's not a story, I know that. I just
mean you shared something with someone, and it was good

for you, but that doesn't mean your entire life needs to change."

I took a deep breath and shivered in the wind, and we turned back toward the road. The breeze off the water was filled with the rattle of leaves, a sound like rain and fire. He took my photos from me the same way he took my body sometimes: without a word.

I'd surrendered to him because I needed something. Wanted something. I wondered now at the way pain could shift, the way it would change color in the light. We walked back to Ruby's apartment, her arm still looped in mine, our hair tangling together in the wind. I was empty as the dead, blameless as the slaughtered.

# 8.

All my days were the same.

He didn't contact me. I spent mornings in my apartment shooting elaborate and busy still lives of flowers and seashells and cracked open eggs. I spent idle nights in the studio. I bought new sheets and a new blanket, more pillows. I started sleeping there even though the heat never stayed on all night. I made hot chocolate and Christmas passed almost unnoticed. I avoided seeing anyone and instead arranged flowers and took photos of my fingers fucking them, spreading the blossoms open, spilling their pollen.

On Christmas Day, I woke up in the studio, snow painting the windows white. I boiled water for coffee, wrapped in a blanket and stood naked on the bed, feeling the cold air touch me. I knew my face was pale in the sunlight, the snow, the roads white with frost. Everything was brittle. I wondered, just to hurt myself, if he thought of this place. If he thought of me. I imagined him getting ready in another city, rolling up his sleeves. I imagined him working, his drawings in his hands, people with dollies and packing crates rolling in the ship of razor light in sections, boxes full of chain and silver, coils of tarnished silvered mirror flowers. I imagined him drinking coffee, focusing on his work with a dark gaze, as he once controlled me, seeking out a necessary beauty.

• • •

One evening, as I returned from the studio, my hair smelling of pearly chemicals and winter cold, I found an ivory envelope on the hardwood just inside my front door. Looking up at me was my name, printed in hyper-neat capitals. I realized I had never seen my name in his handwriting before, but it seemed somehow exactly how I knew it would be, neat and sharp, just like the bite of sorrow on my heart.

Inside the envelope was a slice of thick paper where he printed the date and time of a flight to New York, the booking number for automatic check-in, the confirmation number for a hotel I never heard of somewhere in Brooklyn. There was nothing else. No mention of my photos, not a word about anything between us. He did not even sign his name. Only a cryptic poem of letters and numbers in a neat stack, which would, I assumed, bring me to him when they said so, and not one moment sooner.

I wondered if he would be there.

I wondered if I would.

Even knowing how completely I was taken, taken from, reduced, my heart could not stop its foolish wanting. It continued to amaze me how well and captured I was. I was held with hands and rope, his arms, his teeth. Many times, still slick and breathless, I rested my head on his chest, almost asleep and listened to his heart beating. No matter how many times I heard it, it was always precious and new. I heard it, I told myself holding his letter of letters. Over and over. I listened to his heart race.

In those moments, I thought, his heart believed we were real…

My fingertips could still trace the curve of tattoos along his collarbones from memory. My skin stinging from the bristle of his beard, from the slap of his open hand or his belt. His body, his hands, his tongue: if I closed my eyes, they were still on me, in me, with me. A physical memory is like running a low-grade fever.

Love, desire, passion, the context and weight of these words, too thin for how deeply personal they are. His teeth on my heart. How could I put that away? Solved, like a puzzle. The sexual element was massive, but it wasn't everything. There was another spectrum on which to be satisfied. Love has no true metaphor or comparison in the world outside our bodies.

It carried the quality of a physical pull, intense, already a little sorrowful, self-knowing, a wise, knowing breed of passionate love that lived close to our bodies, our ideas about ourselves. The fact is that I longed to touch his face—to have contact, to feel his skin against my fingertips.

Removing my desire from a question of desire was hopeless.

All I could do was suffer it.


That night I dreamt I was in an airport. White metal columns vanishing into a ceiling of white mist. And there he was, looking up at a departures board, bright white letters, white fields. Wearing his black jacket. In the dream, that jacket was real, perfect, just like the line of his shoulder. All the details were there, and as I watched him, he turned, smiling. Somewhere a flash went off. A shutter sound, played quick, like a guillotine, a metal slide and snap. He was laughing, the white light of a camera flash falling over his face like a sheet. A savage smile sliced across his lips, and he was gone, turning away…already a blur in the bokeh of too bright dream light…

I woke with the sun raining early morning light into my room, my shoulders cold. The sounds outside were different and made me think I was in another city. But I wasn't. I was in my city, cold and alone. I needed to know.

And there it was again, love's desperate foolish pets:

Need and want, and hope.

I checked in to the airline while still in bed, and before I was really sure I was going, I slipped out of the sheets and began to pack. I set aside a set of clothes for the plane, packing identical panties and bras, pants, black sweaters. I took a shower, and my hands only shook a little as I ran a razor over my legs. Anxiety ran down my body with the water. It was done, I realized, soap running down my shoulders, and I began to feel divergent.

Everything before me was happening in split perception. I towel dried my hair, moisturized my skin, pulled on underwear and clothes, finished packing toiletries. My camera. I put a book in my carry-on.

Pristine, sterile like a hospital with all its absent soothing architecture, the airport was a massive white portal that would carry me forward to meet my fate, a thief. The plane took off sharply and tilted in the sky as it sped higher. I felt my blood press flat against the back of my veins and smiled. We flew around a massive stormfront over a dark, choppy span of the lake. The clouds peaked and sharp like an airborne mountain range, the sky looked bruised. The cabin was sleepy and dark. Many people had their window shades drawn.

Flying wide around the storm for almost twenty minutes, hurtling thirty thousand feet above a black span of water, I watched, rapt. In all my life I had never seen anything so powerful, so beautiful. I'd never been in the presence of something so wholly immense.

When the plane landed, the wheels screamed in protest, I could feel the plane try to take off again, lift. The air that rushed in when they opened the door was brittle with cold, and despite myself, despite the weakness of my knees, the trembling of my heart, I smiled.

The hotel room was stark, tucked in a rare cul-de-sac in an older part of the east side, facing a walled garden. Dark grey stucco, its facade was embellished by riotous window boxes of red flowers, clusters of clashing crimson, and ruby, pillar-box red. It looked almost English from the outside; heavy, red-lacquered door, dark rails, black molding and trim.

The hotel felt abandoned, fictional. Even the girl at the front desk seemed half invisible and dreamy. My room had tall windows that opened on a garden, stunning old doors with flat egg-shaped handles. The room was dark grey, with a minimal modern design. The kind of lush white bedding that reminded me with a hard knife-like twist of pain, of our bed, abandoned in our studio.

I dropped my bag by the door, shuffled off my leather jacket, ignoring the hangers and the hooks. I swept my hair out of my face, twisting it into a messy top knot, opened the windows. I set aside my fear and anger, my choking confusion and took a moment to enjoy being there, in a different city. I wondered why he chose this hotel, if he asked for the king-sized bed and the garden view.

It was only standing in the middle of the room, drinking a bottle of sparkling water in long gulps and thinking about ordering a club sandwich from room service, that I realized I had made my choice, id flown all the way here unsure. But now I knew, he sent for me, and I was going to see him,

By some twist of fate, I was hopelessly tied to him, and no matter what happened now, this proved it. I hadn't told anyone I was leaving. I hadn't called my mother or Ruby, I hadn't called my booker, or cancelled the job I was supposed to leave for in two days. I didn't want to feel, of all things, wistful and melodramatic. I had a case against this man, who packed up my soul along with his mirrors, and his books, and his knotted rug. He took my art from me without a word.

I had a case for anger, for rage. But who could have a case against love?

I unpacked nothing; only stripped off my clothes where I stood, leaving them in a black puddle on the floor. In the bathroom, I washed my face and hands, put on a T-shirt and afresh pair of underwear, pulled a robe off a hanger and left it at the foot of the bed. Light the color of pale ice filtered down over me from the headboard as I slipped naked between the sheets, starched and smooth against my skin.

How long had he planned to take my photos?

Why did he take them away....

After lying awake for a long time, I slept, shallow and fitful, I dreamed of walking through a bright living forest.

I visited the gallery in Brooklyn in the early morning. The hour indicated in his note was five hours before the opening listed on the gallery website, but I arrived as instructed, just after dawn, during those hours when the day still feels personal, like maybe it was happening just for me. The gallery was a poured concrete, modern warehouse standing in the middle of a wasted lot. Brutalist lines suggested a bulwark, some kind of Soviet monument with expansive windows and massive copper doors.

The lot was studded with a scattering of rusted metal sculptures of strange animals that could have been dogs or rabbits. Everything was covered in a thin glitter of frost in the dawn. I approached alone, following a desire path through the lot, my shadow cast long and lean behind me, my breath fogging around me like a cloud. The sky was a flat grey steeped in orange that made it hard to tell if it was just after dawn or just before dusk, and it was the kind of bone-cold that made me think of the dead of winter. I curled my gloved hands into fists. The smell of frost lingered in the air. I was so nervous I could hardly breathe.

Soon, I told myself, this day would be over. In a matter of hours. Who would I be when night fell? Would I know myself? Would I recognize her?

The doors were open light, moving at my touch. I was surprised it was open, surprised by the lushness of the entryway, full of light. It felt deserted, empty. I walked around, following the curving cement wall streaked by age and time and a period of neglect. Three vast swathes of blue fabric were draped high overhead, rippling slightly in the air-conditioning, lit up as though they hovered on wind and light, so rich in color they appeared to lack depth and form. Voids of pure hue. I was alone.

The space was silent as a held breath. To the left of the doorway, on a curving wall, was an archway that suggested a hall. It was flickering with pearly frantic light.

I followed this light down the concrete hallway, lined with veils of thin gauze catching the flickering light, shimmering reflections. Light spinning somewhere ahead, splashing against a wall, fractured and scattered and flooding down this hallway, light bouncing, rainbows shattering past like lightning, a tumble bathed in a delicate silver glow. At the end of this flickering hallway was an archway, full of light and bounce. It gave way to a room as open and high as the building itself, a tall echoing silo.

And anchored in space, below the impossibly high ceiling, were my photos. Stark black and white forms hanging from the ceiling like bats, glowing silver, pooling blacks, the layered hands, surreal shapes, punched against the slate grey walls, impossibly at home. silent surreal witnesses to the city of beauty and knives he'd built. The starburst of light, the perfect creation of a random moment of destruction, exposed in all its beauty.

The photos and the statue belonged together.

And the correctness was enough to make me forgive him. No, not forgive. That is too bitter a word. It forced me to understand. Nothing needed to be forgiven.

The mirror shards glittered and glimmered, casting reflections everywhere. Refraction. Memory changed the importance of his piece, my relationship with it. It sparkled in the light, reflections always moving like it was underwater. Reflections were rich and subtle, complex and beautiful, breathing. Alive.

Its shape reminded me, always, no matter how many times I saw it, of a tall flying ship, a sailing castle. Its sharp and lovely angles repeated and reflected countless times over its mirror skin. An infinity of reflections bound to its body in a concrete room, making the air warm and bright, full of light so sharp it was almost a sound. A sensation.

Every movement ricocheted around the sculpture; for a long time, I didn't move, just stood as still as I could and looked at our work. I watched the stillness of light and glass and metal, the endless dancing of reflected light on the walls. The space reminded me of him. As though he touched every surface. I pressed my palms against the cement wall behind me, cold against my skin.

The light pouring out of the heart of the sculpture flicked gently, an almost invisible change. A color shift, a span of lines as the light became not a steady organic glow but a recorded light capturing.

Video.

I wondered for a moment how he did it. Perhaps a tiny screen in the heart of the structure, coiled up with the lights and support chains, the projections bounding off the mirrors, reflections firing over its razor-sharp body like shrapnel. Reflections bleeding to bright white that resolved themselves, with a slightly titillating quality of spontaneity, into a streak black and white view of a hardwood floor. Our studio floor.

My heart lifted, fluttered. I couldn't help it; I lost my breath.

Somehow, I had been filmed in that moment. To late I remembered the little camera inside the sculpture, to film his work. It had captured a strange frame. My chest and throat, my shoulders, my jaw and mouth, the sweep of my cheek and the corner of one of my eyes. Me. An object displayed like one of my photographs. But there was something else as well, an unremarkable beauty, something honest and naked, a heart's simple expression multiplied and a kaleidoscope of shards of a body in motion, in ecstasy, was compelling, altering. A shattered perspective, violent and beautiful. Honest and naked.

In countless frames, my hands travelled over my breasts, my mouth opened, tongue escaping for red seconds across my lip, my breasts folded under my arms, filled the spaces between my fingers. Disembodied hands moved across nipples pulled tightly like flower buds. The tendons under my jaw stood out as I turned my head. A rail of collar bone cast a shadow.

It was more than me. It was a thing of beauty all its own, something that had nothing to do with me or my ideas about me. Something for which I was only a tangential subject, a real thing, an object with none of the complexity of being a person, none of the fog of memory. Only vibrant pleasure, glowing, moving skin.

I stood trying to accept the loss of my self-image, a fantasy I believed was necessary, a hard wall of introspection in a massive public space filled with my body. Just as he told me about pain through the impact of his hands and his belt and his ropes, he convinced me like this; by breaking my idea of my body into a million glittering images. Beautiful.

I was art. An action. It wasn't that he showed me a choice: to see myself as beautiful or look away. He showed me, brutally and abruptly, that it wasn't a choice at all. What is imaginary is untouchable. And then, there is reality: what happens, what has happened, what you know, what you have felt with certainty. And you can't protect yourself from one with the other.

# 9.

And just like before, he wasn't there and then he was.

Standing near me and my body was screaming: eat me, drink me. I was so in love with this, with him. For months, I'd felt this every second and denied it. Denied every proof of what I felt. And somehow, in the face of mostly mute refusal, this is what he offered me. I loved my life with him. I was reduced to the essences, steady contentment.

In the gallery, his piece glittered like a supernova beside us. He walked forward. This is the real lesson I learned again and again; most enormous, fatal things occur in the beat of an eye, the tremor of a voice.

"Kneel."

His voice cracked slightly as he spoke, genuine feeling, and I did not need to tell my knees to bend. I knelt, light casting on the walls around us. Kneeling. Every drop of blood in my body pulled toward him.

"It was you, you know. Always. I knew when I first saw you, watched you. When I thought of the shape of this piece, of the images that would play over it—the perfect obscenity, it was you. I knew it had to be. The girl who came to photograph my Piano."

There was no awkwardness as he approached, not a single glimmer of uneasy self-awareness as he slid to his knees before me and locked me in his familiar gaze, reached out his hands for mine. He held them, and what I'd thought I lost was returned a thousand times. A truth carved into reality, unmistakable, I belonged where the rules were ours. Where the sky over my head was the motion of his hands turning back his sleeves as he stood, towering over me. And his voice was leather.

"And as soon as I touched you, watching the way pain moved through your body, watching your mouth, your hands…"

He shivered, his thumb sliding over my lips.

"When I saw your work." He looked up, holding my jaw in hand. "Such softness and violence."

Different words with the same tone, the same sound and color. His grip was firm, and I belonged inside it. I belonged in the space between never and again, between stop and keep going. Lost in the brilliant frantic wildness of whim and permission.

"You would never let me do this, but I had to do this for you. I'm so sorry."

I was afraid for a long time that I could not speak. How could I tell the sun about all the light I saw when it shone. I only nodded my head and waited.

"Stand, strip, and then kneel again."

I stood, alive with the electric song of want. I dropped my coat to the floor, untied my boots, I peeled off my sweater and jeans, dropping layers until I was wearing nothing but my skin and want. I knelt again, tiled my dead down, my hands open on my thighs, my knees spread. It was cold in the room, silver light flashing, the concrete made me shiver, covered my skin in goosebumps.

He watched every move, and being watched by him made me feel more stripped, more naked, flayed down to the bone, every inch of me waiting and visible. Carefully he reached down with curled fingers and brushed my nipple. I shivered; the impact of the touch exaggerated by context.

I closed my eyes, listening hard for the laughter of clothing falling away, the buttons on jeans, the slide and chime of a belt. Suddenly, pain closed hard around the back of my neck. The pain made it hard to get my breath back. His body forcing me onto the floor, on all fours, pressing harder, harder.

His other hand ran up my thigh, lifting my sex, my ass. He slapped the round of my ass cheek with a hard slap that made me sob in surprise. The sound echoed in the massive space, bright and rising. He spanked me again and again. Every slap was different, soft or hard, a firm hard slap that rolled through me or fast, rapid strokes that snapped like whips and built a quick burning heat inside me.

He fell on me, his cock slid up my thigh. I felt and heard him groan as the head touched the wetness of my sex. I answered with a moan of my own, thrust back to feel more of him. He closed me in his hands, controlling every breath and motion, pulling moans and sighs out of me. Hands around my waist, tight, his fingers dragging into my skin, leaving red marks behind them, he lifted me up so that he could penetrate me in a single vicious thrust that ground his pelvis against my own, my knees almost off the floor.

Again and again, he lifted me toward him, repeated the action, snarling deep in his chest, his grip on my skin a deep singing agony. I closed my eyes to feel him better, better listen to the sound of his cock sliding in and out of the moisture that spilled from me, answering the suddenness of his entry with shameless swelling and arousal. He fucked me so hard my breath gasped out of me.

The hand around the back of my neck gripped my hair and forced me up, arching my back. With his other hand, he smacked the round of my ass, a brutal slap, a single motion. He spanked me hard until my skin felt speckled with pain, sharp and abraded. I cried out then, unable to help myself. Sobbing into the floor.

"I have seen your body; I know it so well." His voice was close to my ear, and then he was gone. His hands gone. My head fell forward, and my arms gave out. He stopped fucking me, stopped spanking me, touching my skin softly.

"I want to feel you." I whimpered into the floor. My eyes closed. I lost all orientation, trembled hard. He passed his hand all over my body, feeling every curve. Passing over and over my sex without stopping, until finally, finally, he did. His palm pressed and still. I trembled, overcome with the impossibility of not grinding my hips against his hand.

"If my hand stays here…" he said, again, so close. "Do you feel it?"

I nodded, panting.

"If my hand stays here, could you come for me?"

I nodded, and he pressed his hand more firmly.

"Closer…" I said, gasping.

He raised his hand and smacked me hard, the lips of my sex singing brightly with pain. A tingling rolled slow up my skin. My heart beat wildly, and I knew he would feel it even in my cunt, pressing me into the floor. He hit me again, pain rocking up my body from my sex to the top of my head. A long shiver. And I sobbed. Still, the orgasm was close, closer. Hovering, and when he hit me again, his hand came away wet, glistening, and I could feel the pleasure this caused him in the snarl deep in his chest. My skin was red, a cloudy purple sky of bruises, and I was crying out into the floor, my tears and sweat rolling down my cheeks.

Hauling me up and turning me around, forcing me on to my back, the floor hard and hot from the flush of my chest, still cold and bright against my ass and thighs, which were alive with pain. He pressed me into the floor with his hand splayed, almost the width of my chest.

He took me again, fucking me hard in the light and shadow of his sculpture. Of my flirting orgasm, flushing chest. He tossed my leg up over his shoulder high so that he could plunge into me and see me at the same time. He wanted to see everything. The film ended.

Now it was only us, reflected in the mirror and glass. His hand closed around my throat, my breath stuttering, stopping. The world pulled away, sound fading to a crushing static. My eyes on his, locked and watching as the world fell away…

Fell away…

And came rushing back. Breaking waves of static and sound, the heave of breath, his cock in its violent home inside me. Static and fear resolved themselves into the sound of his breath, the hard pulse of his orgasm as he held me up to him, returning from the fall, in his arms.

Holding me as he would something precious, moving softly, slowly, in and out of me, and finally, came, a long slow crash of sensation. My body slick with sweat and humming from pain.

"My good girl," he said, falling back, and we were both released. We lay in the sparkling brightness, surrounded by the strange light and shadow of his sculpture. Everything around us dripping with the quality of erotic suggestion. My photos suspended over us like strange constellations. My tears, the ones he wrung out of my skin, burned on my skin. My skin was tender from his brutality. We burned me with the fire inside us, the heart of a wolf, pumping wolf's blood. His hands were like shapeshifters. Like hammers, like stones, like flowers as he stroked my cheek, my heated swollen skin.

I watched him. My heart, my sadist with copper eyes. A man who could consider himself a manager in pain and pleasure.

I thought, *this is happening at the beginning of my life, not the end.*

"Perhaps this is not so different as believing your soul has been captured in the camera," he said softly, looking at my hands. "You take and offer me my soul over and over."

"I have spent most of this last year trying to find a way to I say I love you." I said, finally. Finally.

"Why was it hard?"

"Discovering sensational firsts, living on the sharp edge between the boundaries of myself and oblivion. Maybe I was wrong, maybe I was mad. Maybe everything I was feeling was a high from all the pain and pleasure and when you were done, I would be…"

He bit my palm, the meat of my thumb, and my voice stopped. It hurt. He bit harder, a wide impossible array of sensations scattering over and under my skin like a three-dimensional map of stars. My nervous system blooming with spontaneous light. He gripped my wrist, ground his teeth together so it was all I could do not to wimpier.

"I love you," he said into my hand, into the sore bright red teeth marks on my skin, into my body.

What it is to see a new color, wear new skin. If there is one thing I'm intimate with now, it is my senses, the vividness of pain and love. I have had experiences I do not know the word for because no word in my language exists, so no language shapes them, only sensations. How do you write a sensation? You write a poem, you make a photo or build a sculpture.

"I love you. Every mark I leave you is a love story."

He kissed the bite mark on my hand, already swollen.

# About the Author

Lauren Jane K. is a designer, photographer, and writer from Toronto where they live with their little black cat. They like books, cameras, black sweaters, and 24 hour anything. They put oat milk and sugar in their coffee and create erotic stories & images at laurenjanek.com/

# More from Deep Desires Press

**Prey**
**Britt Collins**

*Most people learn after the first mistake, two at the most. It took Lucas Ford three and now it might cost him his life.*

*Mistake number 1:*
*At eighteen years old he saw the unthinkable, a vampire. She told him her name is Victoria. He followed her through the woods and enviously watched as she drank from another. He fell in love.*

*Mistake number 2:*
*He told other people what he saw. From that moment on Lucas was labeled as crazy. After years of therapy and joining the army he was cured and beautiful, exotic Victoria—and his love for her—it all became a fading dream.*

*Mistake number 3:*
*He let twenty years pass, thinking she was a figment of his imagination. Now she's here and very real and needs his help.*
*Vampires are under attack by a new kind of predator. They are no longer at the top of the food chain. Lucas is determined to find this twisted executioner before Victoria becomes the latest victim.*
*He's more than willing to lose his life for her.*

### His Mate Series
### Charli Mac

*Now available as a bundle! The* **His Mate** *series is a set of fated-to-be-mated PNR novellas featuring shifters, werewolves and demons (Oh my!). We even throw in a witch for good measure. In a world where things go bump (and grind) in the night, our heroes are smart, seductive, and sexy as hell. They're on the hunt for some badass, beautiful and even book-reading heroines. This complete bundle contains all six novellas of the* **His Mate** *Paranormal Romance series.*

*His Curious Mate Anna is sensible, staid, and single—and sick of it. She wants excitement; she wants to be tied down and spanked! How's shifter Callum supposed to say no to that, especially when the woman is his mate?*

*His Cautious Mate Getting tied up by his mate isn't the most conventional start to a relationship, but Gregor has no intentions of going anywhere, not when he's got shy but sensual Bea playing nurse maid.*

*His Capricious Mate Coffin? Seethe master Tobias has a kink dungeon, thank you very much, and he's delighted to give ex-cop-now-artist Cat her own, very personal tour.*

*His Calamitous Mate Daisy is a witch with a problem— Abigor, warrior demon, the Grand Duke of Hell. He's just attached himself to her as her personal bodyguard, key word: personal.*

*His Classy Mate Evangeline is a vampire and lady. That won't stop her from doing what needs to be done to protect human Michael from the malicious intentions of fellow vampire Julian.*

*His Contrary Mate Janna is meant to take a wolf for a mate, not a hapless vampire. Kevin doesn't much care for what should happen, and if he has to take on an entire shifter pack to keep her, he will.*

### Wolf Heart
### Dorian Flynn

*It's been years since Elias has seen his childhood rival and friend Julian. The last time they were together, Elias kissed him, sending Julian running away. And by morning, he was gone. Since then, Elias has kept his secret close to his chest, hoping Julian would do the same.*

*But Julian is back now, and simultaneously a string of mysterious animal attacks have struck the town, rousing superstitions about a Beast that swept through before Elias was even born. A Beast that was only stopped by Elias's grandmother.*

*Elias may have been keeping his own secret, but as he and Julian reconnect, what secrets will he discover about Julian's family...or his own?*